MY BOX-SHAPED HEART

Rachael Lucas

MACMILLAN

First published 2018 by Macmillan Children's Books
an imprint of Pan Macmillan
20 New Wharf Road, London N1 9RR
Associated companies throughout the world
www.panmacmillan.com

ISBN 978-1-5098-3957-5

1 3 5 7 9 8 6 4 2

A CIP catalogue record for this book is available from
the British Library.

Printed and bound by CPI Group (UK) Ltd, Croydon CR0 4YY

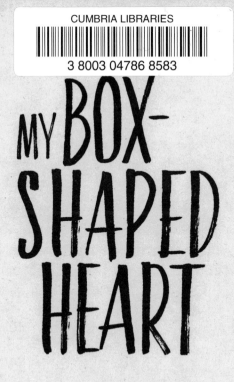

MY BOX-SHAPED HEART

To Rosie, with much love.

CHAPTER ONE

Under the surface, deep in the blue-lit water, nobody can see me.

There's nobody to judge the clothes I wear, or the way my hair frizzles around my head like a halo. I'm wearing a black Speedo swimsuit, which looks like a million others. I'm under here, and when I pull my arms up, gliding and cutting through the surface, it still feels secure.

I count my strokes and revel in my power as I speed from one end of the pool to the other. I regulate my breathing. This is my thing. I have control.

I roll over and float on my back in the water. The sunlight pours through the glass panels in the roof and sparkles across the pool's surface, shooting off prisms of light, which dapple the tiled walls.

Something hits me on the side of my leg and I feel the water sloshing over my face and up my nose. Instinctively I reach out to grab something, but I'm in the middle of the pool and there's nothing there. I bob sideways, like a cork, and my feet stretch down to find the tiled floor. I swipe the water from my eyes and tuck a dripping strand of hair behind my ear.

'Hey.'

The sound is distorted by the echoing acoustics of the swimming pool.

'Sorry – didn't see you there.'

My eyes are stinging from the chlorine. I blink, hard, and the person in front of me comes into focus. I step back reflexively, realizing it's a boy. The resistance of the water makes it hard, and I wobble sideways. It's hard to be graceful when you're up to your shoulders in a swimming pool.

'I didn't spot you under there.' His face is apologetic: eyebrows half raised, mouth in a smile that somehow tugs down at the corners. 'Sorry. Didn't mean to land on your head.'

'You didn't.' I tug at the strap of my swimsuit, looking down. 'It's fine.'

I'm conscious that it's a bit too small and a bit too tight. Generally, I don't stand close enough to other people for them to notice me.

One of the eyebrows lifts up as we stand there for a second, neither of us saying anything.

He's taller than me – which is unusual – and on his head is a wet thatch of dark brown hair. He rakes a hand through it, and there's an awkward moment where neither of us quite knows where to look. That's the moment when the fact that we're both standing in a pool of water, wearing almost no clothes, seems to cross both of our minds at the same time.

I take a breath in. 'OK.'

'Right,' he says. And he jerks his head upward slightly,

in a sort of nod, and steps sideways. I watch as he dives down beneath the water and disappears under the sparkling surface of the pool.

'Holls, my little ray of delight.'

The spell is broken in an instant. As if someone has flicked a switch, the atmosphere changes, and the space fills with the excited gabbling of small children and harried parents. Cressi, the swimming instructor, is beckoning me over. In three long strokes, I traverse the pool and lever myself out.

'You're supposed to use the steps.' Her round face breaks into a mock-admonishing smile. 'If you're going to be leading these youngsters astray before you even get started, we're going to be in trouble.'

I take a step back and look at her, my head cocked to one side. Does she mean –

'I've cleared it with the management. You're in.'

Cressi's our neighbour – or near enough. She doesn't live on our estate, but in a little stone house, which was there long before the housing association came along and filled the fields with row upon row of identical white-clad terraces. She sort of found us, and the next thing I knew she'd whisked me up to the pool where she worked, and now she's offered me the chance to escape on a regular basis. They need an assistant to help with the swimming lessons, and I need a place to go that isn't home.

'Wednesdays are a definite, but can I get back to you about the others?'

I nod. I don't think I can trust myself to speak – mainly

because I can't quite believe that I now have a justifiable excuse for being away from everything, here in the silence and the cleanliness and the space and the clear blue water.

'Excellent. I think you'll love it.' Cressi gives a decisive nod. She sticks her pen behind her ear, and then she hoicks the strap of the swimsuit under her council-issued polo shirt, hefting up her not-inconsiderable bosom as she does so.

If Cressi was an animal, I think to myself as I'm washing my hair in the showers, she'd be a sea lion. She barks – which can be terrifying, until you realize that it's just her posh, public-school background – and she's sort of substantial. Like there's twice as much of her as there is of other people. She owns her space. I like her for that.

I see the boy again afterwards.

The bus stop smells of the chip shop opposite, and my stomach is growling so loudly that the woman standing next to me smiles conspiratorially.

'Those chips smell good, don't they, hen?'

She picks up her bag as the bus groans to a halt and the doors open with a tired sigh. 'No' be long now and you'll be home for your tea.' She motions to the bus, gesturing for me to get on.

'I'm waiting for the 236.'

The door squeaks closed on her reply.

Hopeburn High Street is quiet, the children are all home from school, and the procession of cars full of commuters from the train station hasn't started yet. But there's a

4

queue forming outside the door of the just-opened chip shop opposite, and the warm smell drifts across on the wind. My stomach gives a hopeful rumble.

'Hi.'

I assume that the voice is someone talking on their phone, so I don't raise my eyes from the ground.

I'm still waiting for the bus. I'd text the thing that tells you when the next bus is coming along, but predictably my crappy pay-as-you-go phone battery has died. So I'm just sitting looking at the ground and watching a tiny ladybird making its way along a crack in the pavement.

The smell of vinegary chips hits the back of my nose, but this time it's not on the wind – it's so close that my mouth starts watering and I can feel my stomach contracting. I am ravenous, and the bus is never going to come.

There's a beat of silence, and I realize the voice wasn't on the phone; it was talking to me.

I let my eyes dart up, and as I do I feel the physical presence of the boy from the swimming pool as if it was an actual thing. It's like the air is fizzing, or something.

'D'you want one?'

He's holding a bag of chips, and he shakes it in my direction. He's got a big, open sort of face. Strong eyebrows.

(I have no idea why I've just noticed he has strong eyebrows.)

'No – it's fine, thanks,' I say. I have no idea why I just said that either.

My stomach gives a growling sort of squeak, which is so loud neither of us can ignore it. His mouth (also big) turns down at the corners as he tries not to laugh.

'You sure?'

I reach out and take one, popping it in my mouth and closing my eyes for a split second as the taste of it fills me with delight. I haven't eaten since this morning and I am so hungry that I realize now that the spacey feeling I've had since I got out of the pool is probably lack of energy.

I swallow.

'Thanks.'

'Have some more. I've got loads.'

He perches beside me on the seat so we're almost the same height. He must be over six feet tall. I'm five eleven, so I tower over almost everyone I know. You'd think it'd be hard to be invisible when you're the size I am, but somehow I just sort of blend into the background.

I pull out another chip. I'm aware that he's offered chips, and therefore part of me feels that I ought to have some conversation handy for situations like this, but I have nothing. I'm racking my brains.

I look down.

He's wearing a pair of black trainers, which have the ghost of a hole worn in the toe.

I like that. It makes him seem a bit more real, somehow.

'Do you go to the Academy?'

He's interesting-looking. And he doesn't know anything about me.

'Yes,' he says, and he rakes a hand through his still-wet hair. 'I just started –'

There's a second where he stops, as though he's checking

6

himself. He looks at me sideways and rubs his chin.

'Just started what?'

I turn to look at him properly. I think there's something about being here, in a different place, that is making me act more like the person I think I am in my head, and less like the person I am back home in Kilmuir, even though it's only three miles away.

I don't think I've stood this close to a boy in years, but the weird crackly static I can sense in the air is probably completely in my head and the result of watching one too many cheesy films. And the thing is that as 'meet cutes' go (the bit, in case you're wondering, where girl meets boy, and you know that they're just going to get together), meeting at a bus stop after bumping into each other at the swimming pool would be quite a nice one.

Except this is reality, and I am not cute and ditzy and about to fall over and do something adorable. I am tall, I am a bit fat and I think my nose is weird.

'I go to Kilmuir High.'

He looks blank.

'So by rights,' I continue, thinking aloud about the feud between the two schools, 'you shouldn't be sitting here. And you definitely –' I take another chip and wave it for emphasis – 'shouldn't be giving me your chips.'

He raises an eyebrow slightly, and the corners of his mouth turn down again in that funny half smile.

'But you know that already, right?'

'Yep.' He fiddles with the sleeve of his hoody, pulling it down for a second and then pushing it back up almost straight away. It's a bit short. Or maybe he's just a bit tall. I know the feeling.

'Do you go to the pool often?'

It's his turn to ask an awkward question. It's sort of comforting that even weirdly good-looking boys haven't got a clue how to have a conversation either. And we've got no idea when the bus is coming, so this could take some time.

'All the time.' I hitch my swimming bag on my shoulder as I say it, as if it's just reminded me it's there. 'I'm going to be teaching soon.'

'Cool,' he says. He laces his fingers together and then untangles them. For a weird moment, I have to suppress the urge that my brain – which seems to be doing all sorts of odd things this afternoon – has to make me reach over and touch one of them, just to see if they're warm or cold. I have no idea why. I have absolutely no reference points for this stuff. It's not like I can watch my loving parents being physically affectionate to each other and think, ah – *this* is what it's supposed to look like. I'm just making it all up as I go along, and it's pretty confusing.

'Maybe I'll see you there again?' he says. 'I reckon I'll be going most nights after school.'

'Same,' I say, and he gives me another one of his wide-mouthed smiles. Is he handsome or is he weird-looking? I can't actually tell.

He's sort of both at the same time.

A second later the bus pulls up, and I grab my things.

'You coming?' I ask, fishing my pass out of the front of

my rucksack. I grab the metal rail and turn back to look at him. He's moving in an unhurried sort of way, unfolding his long legs and straightening up.

'Nah,' he says, standing up and pulling up his hood despite the sunshine. 'I wasn't waiting for the bus.'

'Can you two no' have this conversation by text message?' the driver calls out at us from behind the glass, nodding approval as he scans a look at my bus pass.

'I –' I begin, but the door swooshes shut, and I'm jolted as the bus lurches forward. I watch as – I don't even know what his name is – raises a hand in farewell. I flop down into a seat and turn to look back at him. He grins at me as the bus pulls away, down the high street, back to my own life where nobody talks to me and strange, weirdly good-looking boys don't offer to share their chips with me.

'Those seats aren't for you, hen.'

I feel my face going scarlet as the woman opposite me motions to the wheelchair sign. I pick up my bags, and – despite the fact that the bus is empty but for the two of us and two younger boys who are drawing faces on the window in the condensation from their breath – I move. Obediently, and without making a fuss. In my head I point out that if someone got on and wanted the seat, of course I would move. But, like most of the arguments I have with people in my head, it stays there.

We turn the corner out of Hopeburn and head past the castle on the way over the hill. The trees are lime green with leaves, and the sun is shining. It's summer, and the loch is shining blue.

I rest my head against the window and it bumps along as we pass the outskirts of town, rising up to the crest of the hill that leads to Kilmuir. My stomach isn't growling with hunger now; it's lurching with a strange, half-nervous feeling. Am I ever going to see him again? What sort of person just randomly sits down and has a conversation in a bus shelter?

I think back over everything that was said (which isn't that much, I know). His accent sounded more like Edinburgh – definitely not from round here. Maybe that's what he meant when he said he'd just started?

My mum's English, which means I don't sound anywhere near as Kilmuir as the people at school. She was always really particular about me 'speaking properly', as she put it (if you're looking for a way to mark your children out as different, teaching them to speak in a way that everyone considers stuck up is a good start). So we say *yes, darling*, not *aye*; and it's *not*, never *no'*; and you don't ever say *dinnae*. Useful if I was planning a career as a newsreader, I suppose. All it's really done is give me a little extra something – as if I needed it – to make it clear I'm not like everyone else.

I used to daydream about moving house and starting again. In my fantasy, we'd have a huge, spacious white house (when I was ten, I used to pore over the IKEA catalogue and mark my favourite pages) with giant windows and bright light pouring in. It'd look like spring all year round. I'd be minimalist and uncluttered, and nobody would know who I was. When I turned up for school, I could reinvent myself, start afresh.

But that's not what happened. Instead we live here in Kilmuir, where every single one of your mistakes hangs around your neck forever. That's partly why I decided to start swimming at the pool in Hopeburn. Cressi sort of forcibly befriended my mum – it's hard to explain, but that's just how she is – and the next thing I know I was being bundled in the car with her and given a lift to the pool where she worked. And I realized that nobody there knew or cared who I was, and I didn't have to worry about bumping into people I wanted to avoid. There is a pool in Kilmuir, but even though you might be hard to spot in the water there's always the chance that afterwards, hair ratted with chlorine, you might bump into someone from school. So I took Cressi up on her offer, started using my bus pass, and escaped to another world – or the closest I can get to one. I'm aware that exchanging one tiny Scottish town for another three miles away isn't exactly reinventing myself, but there's a limit to how much I can do. I'm only sixteen.

CHAPTER TWO

I've walked this path so many times that I swear my feet know their own way. I feel the gravel of the path crunching through the thin soles of my fake Converse (which are actually quite nice – they've got red flowers all over them), and I run the flat of my hand along the tops of the cow parsley, which is frothing along the verge. I walk past the path that leads down to Cressi's little stone cottage and along the pavement towards the estate. Down the path, through the play area where three little girls are dancing on a makeshift wooden stage they've made out of an old pallet, like I used to with Lauren, when we were sisters.

A picture of her seven-year-old face pops into my head for a fleeting moment, and I remember the day we met for the first time: me on roller skates on the path outside the house; Lauren standing, a too-big pink holdall over one shoulder; and Neil, her dad, giving us both money for the ice-cream van.

And then Neil moved in with mum, and we went from two to four. Our house was my granny's house, and when she died the housing association let us stay there. Over the years, the flowery wallpaper was painted over with bright colours, and the patterned curtains replaced with long cotton ones from IKEA. And Lauren and I crashed up and down the stairs surfing on a mattress and scuffing the walls with our school shoes, and for a while it felt like we were a proper family – the kind you see on the adverts on television. I liked having a stepsister, and I felt happy lots of the time. And Mum smiled a lot then too. Until Neil started disappearing and leaving us at the weekend and saying he was working. And then he'd come back and be all smiles and charm and flowers from the petrol station up the road and they'd share a bottle of red wine from the corner shop and Lauren and I would fight over the television and then one day it all just ended.

Round the corner and past the gardens.

Our house is the second in a long white terrace, the walls spiky with stone harling. I press the flat of my hand against it for a second, feeling the way each little stone jabs into my palm.

When I was little, I fell on my roller skates and crashed into it, head first. I've still got a constellation of scars on my forehead left over from the accident.

I try the door, but it's locked. I fish my key out of my pocket and try to shove it in the keyhole, but the key's in the other side, so I can't do that either. I think about yelling through the letterbox, but decide it's just as easy to go round the back. Our house is so small that when I peer through the dappled glass, I can see straight through it to the fuzzy green of the back garden. I pocket the key and head round the back.

The passage is crammed with a heap of bikes, which

makes me smile. Mine used to be one of them. Before the Academy – before the gang we used to be was divided by some unknown criteria into the cool, the uncool and the unspeakable – we all used to hang out together. We'd hurtle around the pavements, playing football and rounders, and doing bike races and speed skating on the big green along the way. And then it all stopped. These bikes belong to the little kids who used to tag along begging to join in with us – they were four then.

Now they're freckle-nosed nine-year-olds, and I half wish I could join in with their games. It's funny, but growing up isn't anywhere near as much fun as it looks on the Disney Channel.

We don't have a back garden so much as a sort of patch. The grass is a bit long and shaggy, and there are dandelions sprouting up in the corners. I take a handful and shove them in the side of Courtney Love's cage. She hops out, twitching her nose in approval. I like to think the actual Courtney would be pleased to discover there's a rabbit named after her. We used to have a guinea pig too, called Kurt Cobain – but he died. We probably could have predicted that.

The back door's open. I push it – hard – and manage to squeeze through the gap. We've got a sort of little back room – I think maybe it was meant to be for bikes and stuff. But it's not full of bikes and stuff. It's full of . . . everything.

There's a tower of kitchen rolls balanced on top of a stack of newspapers, which were going for recycling until they weren't because they were being saved for something.

There's a pile of bags full of bags, because they're going to go out some day but we might just keep them in case they come in handy. The bookshelf is overflowing, the shelves double-stacked with books, and covered in dust. There's some sort of cross trainer under a heap of black bags, which are full of clothes from when I was little, which are going to be a patchwork quilt. One day. Everything in this house is going to happen on a mythical future date when the planets align, and in the meantime it's as far removed from my tasteful, white-painted Scandinavian dream escape as it's possible to be. I step over a huge crate of Avon catalogues and the kit that came with them. They're dated September 2015. The catalogues weren't handed out. The make-up samples are still encased in their shrink-wrap. One day, I'm sure, they'll make their way to wherever they're supposed to be. In the meantime, they're just another might-have-been, boxed up – just in case – and lying in a pile of all the other stuff that makes up the chaos of our house.

It's not just a bit untidy. It's more than that. We used to live – when there were four of us, and life wasn't unravelling – in a sort of happy muddle. Paintings on the walls, and piles of coats on the end of the banister in the hall. Shoes heaped up under the stairs, and stuff that was going to be tidied up (but never quite made it) in piles on the kitchen worktop.

But that was before. Now it's just the two of us, and the walls are closing in. I thought when Cressi found out what the house was like it might make things change

– that Mum would be embarrassed out of her torpor and into action. But no. And as time passes, and Mum spends more and more of her time shopping online in a dressing gown and watching *Friends* on repeat, it's like the fuller the house gets the emptier it feels. It doesn't make sense.

I try to tidy it up when she's not looking, stacking stuff in piles and filtering through out-of-date stuff. But it causes arguments and she gets stressed out and it's easier to escape to the pool on the bus, or catch a lift with Cressi. And when Cressi asks how things are, or why she hasn't seen Mum for a few weeks, I manage to gloss over it by saying she hasn't been feeling well. Cressi's busy managing the swimming school, and I think she's worked out there's not much point trying to get through to Mum any more. It's happened before with the woman who used to live across the road. Eventually, if you don't get anything back, you stop trying to be friends with someone.

As I walk through the back-room door, I can hear the television on in the sitting room.

'Hi, darling,' calls Mum.

I go inside and find her sitting on the sofa, hands wrapped round a mug of tea, her feet curled up under a blanket despite the fact that it's June and sunny outside.

'D'you want to watch this with me?'

She's watching repeats of *Friends* on one of the Freeview channels. Her hair's tied up in a scruffy sort of bun, and she's still in her dressing gown. I shake my head and reverse out of the room, making an excuse about having to have a shower to wash the chlorine out of my hair. I'll grab something to eat on the way.

I wake up before the alarm goes off and head downstairs.

I step carefully through the minefield of plastic bags and cardboard boxes, piles of washing and unopened letters. I put the kettle on and pick my school jumper up from the drying rack, sniffing it as I do so – I'm paranoid it smells weird, but I can't smell anything but the acrylic of the fabric and a faint odour of Fairy Liquid. I had to wash it by hand last night in the kitchen sink because we've run out of washing powder.

I half hope as I open the fridge that a miracle might have happened overnight, but when I look inside there's still only a dried-up lemon, a piece of cheese that has cracked and gone dry, and the milk carton in the door. I really need to go to the shop.

I shake the milk and realize there's only enough for one cup of tea, so I put the teabag from the second mug back in the jar and pour the water into one. There's the end of the loaf in the bread bin, so I toast it, spread it with butter, and put it on a plate.

When the tea's ready, I take it upstairs with the toast, repeating the precarious journey. I slop some on to a heap of papers in a shoe box and pull a face, but there's nobody there to see it. Whatever it is, it'll dry out. I hope.

'Mum?' I push open the bedroom door with my foot. It resists, and I transfer the mug to my other hand and lean my bodyweight against it. There's a crackle of plastic bags and a slithering noise as the objects behind the door shift, making space for me to tiptoe into the room.

All I can see is a lock of faded henna-red hair sticking up from under the naked duvet. The clean covers I left there the other day are still folded up on the floor, and she's sleeping on the bare mattress.

'Mum.' I lift the corner of the duvet and shift her alarm clock round so the red numbers are shining in her face.

'Off,' she mumbles.

'It's eight o'clock,' I say. I shove an empty box of paracetamol off the bedside table to make space for the mug, balancing the plate with the toast on top.

'I'll get up in a minute.'

I'll be going in a minute. I don't let the feelings in. The only way to cope is to take a deep breath and just let it go over my head. She can't do mornings – she never could. But especially not now. I turn to leave.

'Holly?'

I have my hand on the door. I lift my head and tuck my hair behind my ear.

'Mmm?'

'Love you, darling.'

'I know.' I make my way back across the room and kiss my fingers and put them on the duvet, approximately where her head should be.

'I'll be up later, I promise. I just need to have a bit more sleep, then I'm going to get things sorted.'

'OK.'

I've heard that a million times. Sometimes I get home

and there's a pile of black bin bags by the front door where she's started clearing up, but inevitably I find her, slumped on the sofa with a cup of tea watching the shopping channel, or dozing. She starts off with good intentions, but she just gets tired halfway through. It's as if she can't quite work out what to throw away and what to keep, and it's too tiring to figure out. So she just gives up.

And we live on in this house, as it silts up slowly with layer after layer of random stuff.

'Mum?'

I call up the stairs. There's no sound.

'I'm leaving now.'

There's a vague mumbling.

'Try and eat something,' I say, and pull the door closed behind me.

School is . . . school. I hover around the edges of it. I'm basically invisible, which is better than it sounds. I don't get into trouble. I don't get picked on by anyone. Teachers don't single me out to read aloud in class. In fact, sometimes I wonder if I'm there at all. I swear it's like I wear an invisibility cloak. I was standing in the corridor last week when Lauren and her friends walked past, talking about Jamie's party. She didn't even acknowledge my presence. As time passed after our parents split up, she drifted further and further away, snared by the sharp-edged cool-girls gang, who were impressed by the big house she lived in and the expensive car Neil drives now.

And so these days Lauren and I don't really talk to each

other at school. I'd say we're not in the same social group, but my social group is the weird collection of misfit people who end up sitting at the same table at lunch every day, not really saying anything. I sometimes wonder if I went somewhere else and started again, would I still end up sitting at the same table, just in a different school?

There's one thing different about today. Halfway through maths, I feel myself grinning, and I look down at the page before anyone notices. I remember the look on the boy's face as I turned round to look at him, surprised.

I wasn't waiting for the bus.

CHAPTER THREE

I get home from school and the house is silent.

'Mum?'

She must be asleep. Again. I got up to go to the loo at three am, and the light was still on in the hall downstairs, so I bet she's either gone back to bed for a nap or she hasn't been up since. I look up at the clock on the wall – no, she can't still be asleep. She must be . . .

'Holly, honey, is that you?'

Her voice is small.

'Mum?'

I make my way through the hall and up the stairs, and she's lying there in the doorway of her room. Her leg is twisted at a weird angle, and her face is tiny and pinched with pain.

'I couldn't reach the phone.'

I feel a sickening wave of guilt wash over me, right through my whole body.

'What have you done? How long have you been here?'

She exhales, her breath making a shaky sound in the silence. 'Maybe an hour or two. I think I bumped my head.'

I dart a look at her, leaning in close to peer into her eyes. They look normal, but . . .

'I need to call you an ambulance.'

'No.'

Her nostrils flare – I'm not sure if it's pain or anger, or maybe it's both. She tries to shift herself sideways, but her hip knocks against the bottom of a stack of shoeboxes and they start to topple. I reach out and steady them before they fall on top of her, and the lid of one of them dislodges, revealing its contents. It's full of ancient-looking pieces of paper; something to do with the bank – I can see the familiar logo at the top. The date says August 2009.

'I've been meaning to sort them,' she says, giving me the look I recognize. It's the look that says *please let's not have that conversation now*. In other houses, it's the other way round – the parents telling the children to clear up – and I feel a wash of shame and something uncomfortable passing over me. Our life is locked away in boxes. I shove the lid back on the box and I know my cheeks are stinging red with the awkwardness of it all.

'It's fine,' I say.

'Give me a hand up. I'm going to get this place sorted. This is the final straw.'

She reaches out a hand for me to pull her up but, although I'm tall and pretty strong, she's taller still – and she's heavy. My pulling isn't doing much because her body is protesting instead of cooperating.

'Mum, seriously, you can't move.'

'No.'

If I was the grown-up, I'd pick up the phone and call for help. But I'm not. I'm in a sort of half-state where I'm not one thing or the other. I have to be responsible for stuff, but she gets the final say, and there's nothing I can do.

And I know what's wrong. If an ambulance comes and sees the state of our house, she's worried that I'll be taken away. But I don't think it works like that. I don't think they just take you away because the walls are lined with things for a rainy day and emergency tea bags and enough stuff to keep a family of six going for a year.

'If I can just . . .' She rolls herself over the other way this time, away from the precariously balanced shoeboxes of stuff, her body sliding on the papers that are lying on the floor. 'There.'

She lifts her good leg up so she can press her foot down and reaches her hand up again to me where I'm standing in the hall, surrounded by years of assorted things that might be useful one day. I heave and she pushes against the floor, and there's a sickening moment when her face goes a horrible whitish-green with pain and she lets out a gasp involuntarily. Seeing it makes me feel sick, so I can't imagine how she feels.

Mum leans against the white-painted banister, her head bowed. Her forehead is beaded with sweat, and her hands are curled into fists, nails digging into her palms.

I know she needs help, and I know she's going to resist every way she can.

'What about if we get a taxi?'

Her ankle must be broken. She's standing on one leg, the other one held up in the air slightly like an injured animal.

'I haven't got any money on me.'

'It's fine. I've got that twenty pounds Neil gave me in my room.'

I'd hidden it away ages ago, planning to spend it on something nice. But when you don't have money there's something about getting some that leaves you frozen and indecisive.

I can hear Mum's breath coming in tight little puffs. I slip past her and into my room. I don't have lots of stuff. My dressing table is as neat as the rest of the house is chaotic. I lift up the china horse and take the money out from underneath – there's a little hole where I've stuffed the note, folded and folded over again until it's a bulky little square. I shake it out and brandish it at Mum.

'I don't know how you're going to make it down the stairs.'

'Just ring the taxi,' she says, and her jaw is set tightly. 'I'll work that out.'

I know the number off by heart – we don't have a car – and ring it from the home phone, which is, miraculously, sitting on the windowsill in the hall. Sometimes it goes missing for weeks on end, lost in the maelstrom of random stuff that fills every surface.

When I look up, I see that Mum is shuffling down the stairs on her bum, her leg sticking out in front of her, mouth twisted up in pain.

'Can I help?'

She shakes her head.

I shove the coats from the end of the banister on to the

chair under the stairs, where they slide off and fall in a heap. They'll have to wait. When we get back, I'm going to sort this place out properly.

The taxi arrives just as Mum hits the bottom step. I stick my head out and hold up two fingers, mouthing 'two minutes' at the driver.

'I don't want him coming in here and helping,' says Mum unnecessarily.

There's not much chance of that. He's on his phone, scrolling with one hand, his other arm out of the window holding a cigarette. The cab is going to stink, and the smell of cigarette smoke makes me heave.

We make a sort of tripod shape. Mum leans heavily on me, and we make it to the taxi, where she hops and shuffles on to the front seat. I slide it back, ignoring the taxi driver's raised eyebrows, and pass her the seatbelt before closing the door and getting in the back.

The taxi driver's clearly decided it's an emergency. We hurtle along the shore road towards the hospital, past the weird, otherworldly shapes of the oil refinery. The air is thick with the chemical smell from the thick plumes of smoke that belch from massive chimneys. And then we're at A&E, and for a second I feel anxious because he's parked us right outside the door. We're not meant to be there and someone's going to say something and I can feel a wave of anxiety building.

'Here you are, hen.' The driver's found a wheelchair, and, clearly feeling important now, he's hefting Mum out of the seat and into the chair. 'Just pull that lever – that's the brake – and you'll be sorted.'

I pull the twenty-pound note out of my pocket, and he gives me a tenner back.

'Give me a ring when you're done, and I'll see you's back – if my shift's no' over, that is.' He shakes his head and looks inside. The waiting area is crowded with people. 'Mind you, by the looks o' that, you'll be a wee while.'

But we're not. The triage nurse takes one look at Mum's face and wheels her through to a room where he takes some details. Mum's henna-red hair flops forward over her eyes. I twist the hem of my T-shirt absent-mindedly while the nurse taps some details into the computer.

'You might have a bit of a wait at X-ray, but the shifts have just changed, so we'll see what they say.'

He looks up at me.

'Your mum's lucky to have such a sensible girl.'

I don't say anything. I just duck my head and let go of the twisted hem of my T-shirt that's now been stretched out of shape. I pull the band out of my hair, shaking it out so I catch a sudden whiff of the chlorine from the pool, and tie it back in a ponytail. And I remember the boy and the bus stop. It feels like a million years ago, and I look up at the clock on the wall. It's half seven. I've got a mountain of revision to do for a science test and literally no idea when we're going to get out of here.

After waiting for an X-ray (Mum, spaced out on painkillers, lying on a trolley in a corridor; me sitting on the floor because there's nowhere else to go), we find out she's cracked a bone that I can't remember the name of,

26

and they put her in a temporary cast.

I call the taxi firm, expecting someone else to turn up – but it's the same driver. He helps Mum-and-crutches into the car, pushing the seat back as far as it'll go so her leg can stick out and not get damaged. I sit wedged behind him, the smell of lemon car freshener mixing with the whiff of stale smoke from his clothes making me feel even more carsick than normal.

'D'you want a hand inside, darlin'?'

He hoists Mum up. She pulls down her top, which has rucked up, and wobbles slightly on the unfamiliar crutches. This is going to take some getting used to. I'm already working out how best to clear a space for her to get to the sitting room, and thinking about where she's going to be most comfortable sleeping.

'We'll be fine, won't we, Holly?' Mum's voice sounds fuzzy round the edges with pain, and painkillers.

I nod. We always are.

By the time I get her inside, tell her to stand still for a moment while I clear a path so her crutches don't slip on a heap of magazines and send her hurtling to the floor with a second broken ankle, I'm already mentally calculating how early I can get up to do my revision.

I plonk Mum on the sofa, grab armfuls of magazines and papers, and shove them on top of the sideboard. The coffee table is still piled up with stuff, but it'll have to wait until tomorrow. Maybe if I get up early enough, I could sort it a bit before school.

'Holly?' Mum looks up at me. She's got shadows under

her eyes so dark they look like bruises.

I sit down carefully beside her on the sofa. 'Uh-huh?'

'Love you, honey.'

'I know.'

'The most.'

'More than that.'

I bob sideways, nudging her with my shoulder. We've always said it, ever since I can remember. She might be tired and frazzled and a bit broken, but she's the only mum I've got.

CHAPTER FOUR

There's a brief moment of calm after my alarm goes off before I remember what's happened. I'm about to get dressed for school as usual, tiptoeing so I don't wake Mum up, when I suddenly remember. She's not lying under the duvet in a heap. She's downstairs on the sofa with her leg propped up on cushions.

I shrug on my dressing gown and make my way downstairs through the teetering piles of stuff. A plastic-clad magazine slips down the stairs in front of me, sliding to a halt when it hits the wall at the bottom, joining several others that have had the same fate. None of them have been opened – it's a music magazine she subscribed to at some point, but they're months out of date now, and have never been read. I bend down to push them into a stack so at least they're out of the way and—

'AAAARGH!'

'Holly?'

I jump back, heart pounding, and sit on the stairs, shaking both hands rapidly.

'What's going on?' There's a thump and a muttered curse. 'This is impossible,' I hear her saying. A second later, there's a clattering, and another thud.

29

'Spider,' I say, recoiling and bum-shuffling up another step.

Not just any spider, either. One with a proper body and sturdy, I-mean-business hairy legs. My back squirms at the thought of it sitting there waiting to get me.

'I'd love to help,' Mum says . . . and I remember again.

I slither down the stairs, and edge my body sideways round the newel post as if my life depends on it, which it quite possibly does, given that the house has been invaded by flesh-eating tarantulas.

Her crutches have fallen down, one in one direction, and the other under the coffee table. I can see straight away that this is going to be way harder than it would normally be, because our house is so full of crap that I have no idea how she's going to get from A to B without falling over something and breaking her other ankle.

'I'll get you some tea.'

Before I go to the kitchen, I put a couple of cushions on the coffee table (shoving a load of stuff off to one side to clear a space) so she can prop her leg up.

'Can you get me some painkillers as well? I can't believe they're expecting me to deal with this with just a couple of ibuprofen.'

By the time I've found some microwave porridge hiding in the back of the cupboard, sorted out tea, cleared a path to the downstairs loo, helped her on to her crutches, and got her back through to the sitting room, I realize there's no way I'm going to make the school bus. Throwing on my clothes, I remember that – to top it all – I haven't done any revision for the science test.

I'm going to have to walk, and I'm going to be late.

'I'm sorry, darling,' she says.

'I've made you a flask of coffee, and there's some oatcakes in the tin.' I put it down on the table in front of her. 'I'll just go in for the test this morning, then tell them I've got a hospital appointment this afternoon.'

Mum looks up at me and pushes a stray lock of hair out of her eyes. For a moment I think she's going to tell me that, no, I need to stay at school, and not to worry, she'll sort something out. But then I watch as her face seems to flatten somehow, and the blank, emotionless expression is back.

'Are you sure?'

'Of course.' I lean down and give her a kiss on the cheek. 'I'll see you later. It'll be fine.'

I know it's not my job to make her feel better. I'm not even completely sure when the roles were reversed. I haven't got time to think about it now anyway – the bus has gone, and the streets have that weird emptiness they have in the between time before school starts. Lateness hangs in the air. I walk as fast as I can, breaking into a jog now and then.

'You're late.'

Predictably, because this is me we're talking about, I can't just sneak in through the school office, make up an excuse and head to class. Instead I walk straight into Mrs

Lennox, the head teacher. I tower over her, but she's still terrifying. I try to think of an excuse.

'I –'

'Is that the best you've got?' She shakes her head, lips set in a tight line. 'This isn't the first time, Holly. I think we need to have a little chat with your head of year about what's going on.'

'My . . .' I scrabble around for an excuse. 'My rabbit escaped.'

She raises her eyebrows slightly and tilts her head to one side. 'Is that so?'

I nod. 'And we live near the road, and I was worried she'd get out of the garden.'

Her eyes raise skywards. She's not convinced.

'Why don't you join me at the end of the day, and we'll discuss this. Three thirty, my office.'

I nod my head obediently.

'Now get to class. Haven't you got a test this morning?'

Talking to her has made me even later. By the time I get to class, everyone's at their desk, heads down, in total silence, working through their test papers. I can't even remember what we're supposed to have learned. I push the handle down carefully, hoping it won't squeak too loudly.

Everyone looks up as I open the door. Mr Gregory tuts.

'Not a word, please.' He puts a finger to his lips.

Allie, the girl who sometimes shares the same table as me at lunch, looks up, catches my eye and grins.

After class, she catches up with me, tapping me on the shoulder.

'Hey. D'you want to come and hang out at break with me and Rio?'

I look at her and suppress the urge to check around to make sure she's not talking to someone else.

We get a coffee from the vending machine – it's vile, and tastes more of hot plastic and sugar than anything else, but our lunch tokens cover the cost of it, so it's essentially free – and we go and sit on the wall underneath the library corner, shaded by the trees.

'Bad morning?' She tucks her hair behind her ear and looks at me sideways before checking her phone.

'Something like that.'

'I can't wait for this bloody term to be over.'

'What's this?'

There's a thud as Rio launches his bag over the wall and sits down between us. He reaches across and takes Allie's coffee before she has a chance to object.

'Gerroff!'

She grabs it back, but not before he's taken a huge swig.

'That is spectacularly disgusting coffee.'

'I rescued Holly. She's had a bad morning.'

Rio nods. He scuffs the toe of his shoe in the gravel, tracing a circle. 'This place is hellish.'

We spend the rest of break talking about Allie's plan to spend as much of the summer in Edinburgh as she can. Rio's dad – who I always assumed was some sort of hippy farmer – is actually an artist, and he sells his work at a gallery in town. It's weird, because I don't really know them, but it's quite comfortable sitting there listening to them rambling away. When the bell rings, Rio and I walk up to geography together, and I watch Lauren – standing alone, waiting outside her maths class – giving me a curious look and a half-wave as we walk by. It feels good not to be the one hovering on the edges for a moment.

One late mark, a run-in with the head teacher, a completely failed test and a lecture about taking my responsibilities seriously now I'm in S5, and I'm heading back to the office.

'If you want time off for a hospital visit, you're supposed to produce a letter,' says the woman behind the glass of the reception desk.

'I've left it at home.'

'No letter, no hospital,' she begins.

I think of Mum lying in the house, and my stomach clenches in panic.

'I have to go,' I say.

She shakes her head disapprovingly. 'This time, I'll let you go. But I want that letter in tomorrow, OK?'

I nod, hitching my bag over my shoulder. I'll work out the details later.

It's not until I'm home, helping Mum to the loo – she's waited all morning because she couldn't face trying to get there alone – that I remember I'm supposed to see Mrs Lennox after school.

CHAPTER FIVE

I've just made it home when I get a text.

Are you en route? C

It takes a second for me to work out who C is, and why an unfamiliar number is texting me. And then I go cold. This is officially the Day from Hell. Not only have I screwed up the test, been late for school, missed a summons by the head teacher, but now I'm sitting in a onesie on the couch when I'm supposed to be at the pool signing the forms for the swimming assistant training course. Shit. Cressi's going to kill me.

I look across at Mum, who is dozing on the sofa, her head leaning against a floral-patterned cushion. Her face is pale, and even though she's sleeping, she still looks like she's in pain. Wake her and tell her I'm going on the bus, or make an excuse? (Another excuse?)

She shifts slightly, and I watch her forehead crease. I can't leave her.

I'm sorry – Mum is sick, I type, and look at it for a second.

Then I look at the jumble of stuff on the floor and the piles of stuff lining the edges of the room and think of the gigantic spider that's living in the hall under the

35

mountains of everything. And I delete it.

I'm sorry – I got sick.

My phone buzzes as I go to put it down on the arm of the chair.

:) No probs. Will drop form in later.

Shit.

CHAPTER SIX

I sit waiting for the doorbell to ring.

Cressi's seen the house before, and she's cheerfully unfazed by the total chaos. She makes her way into the hall, brandishing the forms I need to fill in, a pen in one hand.

'Let's just sort this out.' She lifts up a pile of washing and moves it off the table in the hall to make a space for the paper to go. A cardboard box full of goggles ('Are you going into business?') topples over as she does so, and they spill all over the bags of stuff that are lying on the floor. 'What's this? Washing?'

I can feel my cheeks stinging pink with second-hand embarrassment. 'Stuff for the charity shop.'

'I'll take that, shall I?' She scoops it up capably and hands me the pen. 'Just need your date of birth, that sort of thing – fill it in there, and I'll get it sorted with the office staff . . . Fiona out?' She peers along the narrow hall.

I lower my voice in the hope it'll be catching. 'No – she's sleeping.'

'Already?' She looks at the clock in the hall. 'Half seven's a bit early for an early night, isn't it?'

I don't say anything. I just fill in the form and hand her back the pen.

'Holly?' I hear Mum's voice as I'm turning to open the door and shoo Cressi back out into the pale evening sunshine.

'Aha,' says Cressi, and before I can stop her she's dodged the assault course of random stuff that silts up the hall and headed to the sitting room.

'How're things?' I hear her saying in her cheerful, no-nonsense way. And then, 'My goodness, we have been in the wars.'

Mum says something I can't catch, and I'm surprised to hear them both laughing.

'Stick the kettle on, Holly,' she calls through. 'I want to hear the whole story about what's going on.'

An hour later, we've been organized by Cressi. She's tried her best to get us to come and stay in her cottage – Phil, her husband, is away with work, and there's plenty of room – but Mum is determined she's staying put.

'Well,' Cressi says, and her usual brisk tones are softer and kinder than usual. 'Maybe if you're sure you want to stay here, you'll let me and Holly sort the place out a bit?'

Mum sighs and rolls her eyes. 'It's fine the way it is.'

'Fiona –' Cressi pulls a face – 'on what planet is this fine?'

She puts a hand on a stack of books, which is balancing on top of a pile of black bin bags, which are stuffed full of . . . I don't even remember what they're stuffed with,

38

come to think of it, they've been there so long. I look at the room through her eyes for a second, and I realize that we can't carry on like this.

'I'll help,' I say.

Mum doesn't look particularly happy about it, but she's stuck – literally – so there's nothing she can do. Maybe breaking her ankle is the best thing that could have happened to her, in a weird sort of way.

Cressi's house smells of log fires, even in summer. And the lemony scent of the geraniums on the windowsills. And faintly of dogs. The cottage has been there for more than a century, and it sits, square and solid, in a patch of garden, which is full of tumbling flowers and strange structures made of bamboo poles with sweet peas climbing up them.

'Bin bags,' she says, dumping them in my outstretched arms. 'Bleach, IKEA bags for recycling stuff, kitchen spray.' She plonks them on me – I'm standing in her kitchen while she thinks aloud.

'Are you sure you want to do this now?' I look at the clock. 'It's quarter past eight.'

'Do you have something better to do?'

I shake my head.

'Right.' Cressi gives a decisive nod. 'Then we'll get started. To be honest I hadn't realized how bad the place had become.' She beckons for me to follow her outside.

Until the last few weeks, when she had reached the point when she was spending most of her time in bed, Mum had always managed to head Cressi off at the pass, meeting her for a coffee in town, or joining her for a walk to the woods with the dogs. We haven't had anyone round for ages, come to think of it. Lauren used to turn up now and then, but she's got her own life now, and I just hover round the edges of it at school.

'Saw that chap you were chatting to in the pool today.' Cressi looks at me sideways, pulling the boot of the car open.

I dump the armful of cleaning stuff in, on top of a dog-hair-matted blanket and a pile of old boots, and make a non-committal noise. At least I hope that's how it sounds. Inside I'm dying to ask her more.

'I think he was hoping you'd be around. He looked like he was keeping an eye out for someone.'

I feel a swooping sensation in my knees. I think I'm probably blushing.

'Anyway,' she says, slamming the boot shut and brushing down her trousers in a brisk sort of manner, 'I told him you'd be around sooner rather than later.'

Oh my God. Now it's a thing. It's real.

'Come on,' Cressi says, beckoning me back into the house for a moment.

I look around her kitchen at the shiny metal range cooker and the matching tea towel and oven gloves hanging neatly on shiny aluminium pegs. Even the dogs' bed looks plump and comfortably inviting, and I half wish I could just persuade Mum to come and stay here until her leg is better. I wonder what it'd be like to live in a house where everything is tidy and finished and done. And I'm wondering, too, why Cressi doesn't mind the way our house looks. But I don't know how to ask.

She closes the dogs in the kitchen. I catch a glimpse of my reflection and realize that Mum's not the only one with dark shadows under her eyes.

The other day at school, I was pulled out of class so Mr Taylor could ask if everything was OK at home, Holly, because we're not trying to intrude, we just want to make sure, and we've noticed you've been a bit late with your last two pieces of homework, and . . .

It's midnight by the time Cressi and I stop clearing up. It's not immaculate, but it's better than it was. There's a clear trail to the downstairs loo, the kitchen surfaces have nothing on them, the towels have been sorted out and stacked in the airing cupboard (well, on one shelf . . . the other one is jammed with emergency loo roll and seven boxes of bleach, which probably shouldn't be in there in the first place).

'You, young lady, need to get yourself to bed.' Cressi opens the door to my room. 'Look at the state of this place.' She's teasing. 'Appalling.'

My room is the only one in the house that doesn't look the way the others do. The bed's made. My little ornaments are still on the dressing table. My slippers are paired on the rug beside my bed. And my science books – Oh, God. The homework.

'Now you get yourself off to sleep, and I'll finish making up the bed downstairs for Fiona tomorrow when you're at

41

school. She can sleep on the sofa tonight.'

I set the alarm and get into bed, obediently. After a while, I hear Cressi letting herself out, and the house falls silent. I can hear the mumble of the television from the sitting room as I lie there with my eyes closed, trying to get to sleep. Mum doesn't like sleeping in silence, so she always has the radio or the television playing.

I realize, as my eyelids feel heavier and heavier and my body starts to drift off, that something has to change. Not just for me, but for Mum. We can't carry on like this any longer.

CHAPTER SEVEN

I wake up to the smell of bacon and the sound of someone singing off key. For a second it pulls me back to the way things used to be, and I half expect to hear Lauren crashing around in the room next door and the sound of Neil singing to himself as he shaves in front of the bathroom mirror. Then, as I shift myself upright, putting my feet on the rug and grounding myself, I remember that isn't our life any more.

'Holly, are you up?'

It's Cressi that's calling up to me, not Mum.

'I've made you a bacon roll.'

I look at the clock and feel a jolt of horror. It's eight o'clock. I must've slept through the alarm. Mum's been downstairs all that time and she might've needed me and –

I don't have time for a shower. I run a brush through my hair and shove on my uniform, pull the covers up on the bed, and head to the bathroom where I wash my face and scrub it dry with a towel.

For a moment, looking at the pale, freckle-spattered face staring back at me, I wish we didn't have a no-make-up rule at school and I could layer on foundation and

43

concealer, hide the purple shadows under my eyes, cover my pale eyelashes with black mascara. But we do. So I go downstairs, looking like a sandy-coloured ghost of myself.

Cressi's clearly been here some time. The kitchen has been tidied, and there's a loaded black bin bag on the floor, and another spilling over with catalogues and junk mail, which is already almost full. The room smells sharp and lemony, a cleaning-product scent, which mingles with the smell of cooked bacon and feels comfortable and homey.

'Sit,' she says briskly, as if I'm one of her Labradors.

'I need to check on Mum.' I turn, with my hand on the chair.

She gives me a warning look.

'She's asleep. The painkillers have zonked her out. No bad thing if you ask me. She's got a lot of sleep to catch up on.'

With a firm hand on my shoulder she sort of presses me down into the chair.

I'm not used to being organized. I've been the organizer for so long that I've forgotten how it feels.

'Brown sauce or tomato ketchup?'

I point to the brown, and Cressi gives me a conspiratorial wink. 'Good choice.'

She squeezes it on to two rolls and sits down beside me at the little round table. She looks completely out of place in our house. She's all pink cheeks and healthy walks in the countryside, and this room feels stale and small and airless. But she looks quite happy. It's weird.

'Eat up,' she orders. She takes a mouthful of tea and

looks across at me. 'Your mum's going to need to go back to the hospital today and have that temporary cast taken off. They'll replace it with a lightweight one – or a boot, if she's lucky – and she's going to be on crutches for a good while.'

I nod. 'I've been thinking. I can't really do the swimming thing with all this going on.'

As I was brushing my teeth, I'd realized it, and that I'd need to focus on being there for Mum. It was the right thing to do. I'd swallowed back the tiny little pang of regret that I felt, knowing that meant my chances of ever bumping into Mystery Pool Boy were pretty much non-existent.

'Oh yes you can,' says Cressi. 'You're not getting out of it that easily.'

'What about Mum?'

I think about her lying on the sofa fast asleep.

Cressi swallows a mouthful of bacon roll and wipes her chin.

'She'll be a lot more mobile once they've put it in a proper cast. And I've told Fiona often enough – I'm her friend. That's what I'm here for. To be honest, I'm thinking this broken ankle might be the making of her.' She raises her eyebrows. 'She's going to have to let me get her organized. By the time she's back on two feet, I'll have this house sorted, we'll get her out and about, and she'll be back to herself.'

And for a second it feels like it actually might be possible. Cressi's so dynamic that it wouldn't surprise me if she could turn this place back into a home.

*

I'm not used to getting a lift to school. I actually feel a bit nervous about it, as if it's somehow going to draw attention to me. As we turn down the long straight road that leads to the Academy, my stomach is twisting in knots. I'm trying to work out how to say to Cressi that I don't want her to drop me right outside the front door, but weirdly, as if she can read my mind, she pulls up behind a white van that's parked on the road opposite the school field.

She turns round to look at me.

'I'm sure you don't want me ruining your street cred.' She chuckles to herself.

'I don't think I have any to ruin.'

I pick up my bag. I've just realized I've left my phone charging next to my bed – not that it'd make much difference because I still don't have any data. But even so –

'Will you call the school if there's any problem with Mum?'

Cressi pushes her sunglasses up on her nose and looks thoughtful.

'Fiona will be absolutely fine. I'm taking her up to the fracture clinic. And we'll get that house sorted. It's time enough that you were focusing on being a teenager and getting yourself into trouble and not on keeping things going at home.'

I feel awkward and bite at the skin on my thumb. Cressi switches off the ignition. 'You focus on school and being sixteen. I'll sort this stuff out. That's what friends are for.'

For a second I feel like I could burst into tears. My eyes prickle and I feel a lump in my throat that I can't swallow. I don't even know why.

I get out of the car and wave goodbye as she zooms off, back up the hill to our house.

Our school was rebuilt ten years ago after the old one started collapsing one summer holiday. It's probably the poshest thing in our town, with glass that sparkles in the sunlight and the sort of view across the water to the mountains that would make your average American tourist swoon. Before class, though, the walkway that overlooks the amazing view is filled with little groups of people who haven't made it into the common room. I notice Lauren and her friends before they see me.

It's a weird situation. When we were sisters, I used to walk to primary school with Lauren every day. We'd share a table at lunch, and share secrets at night. We didn't have the same core group of friends, but there was a sort of Venn diagram where we met in the middle. But it feels like over the last few months, we've gone from politely friendly to . . . Well, I get the feeling she doesn't want to be tainted by association. I hitch my bag up on my shoulder and hope that I can slink past her group and skip the whole butterflies-in-my-stomach anxiety thing. I'm too tired to deal with it today.

In among her group of friends, I spot Lauren leaning against the wall. She pushes herself upright and starts walking beside me as I pass.

'You OK?'

I dart her a look of surprise. 'Fine.'

I can feel prickles of sweat beading on my forehead. It's sticky and clammy outside, and I feel like I'm melting in my uniform.

I'm surprised that Lauren's actually talking to me. Half the time she tries to act as if she just hasn't noticed I'm there. It . . . I'd like to say it doesn't hurt, but it does. It feels like my whole life was dismantled, piece by piece. I had a sister; then I didn't. I don't know how to say to her that I miss her.

'How's your mum?'

I look at her again for a moment and try to decide – I can't face telling her about Mum now, not when she's got all the usual suspects hanging around. I try to keep a low profile so they don't have anything on me. It's worked so far.

'She's fine.'

'Tell her I said hi.'

'I will.'

The thing about Lauren is I'm conscious that she knows. She knows the state of our house and what it's like. She comes to visit Mum and has to shove piles of stuff to one side to make a cup of tea, and she knows there might be milk and biscuits, or there might be nothing much to eat.

I feel a pang of guilt. 'Lauren?'

She turns back as she's walking up the corridor to join the others. 'Yeah?'

I shake my head. 'Never mind.'

I see Madison's head pop up like a meerkat – she's the one who makes me feel seriously uncomfortable.

Unfortunately she's also Lauren's best friend.

'Holly?' Lauren cocks her head to one side. 'What's up?'

'Nothing,' I say, and out of nowhere I feel like I could just burst into tears.

Lauren opens her mouth to say something.

I'm torn between giving her a warning look and worrying that it might alert them to something. She's not anywhere near as much of a bitch as her friends are, but when she's with them she adopts a rock-hard carapace. It's the only way to survive.

Madison's eyes narrow slightly as she looks at me. Her ability to sniff out weakness is phenomenal. If anyone finds out about Mum, I'll –

There's a moment where I can see Madison contemplating what to do – she's the cat, and I'm the mouse, frozen to the spot, not sure if she's about to strike.

Lauren flicks a glance at me, tucking her long blonde hair behind her ear. There's a split second when our eyes meet, and I wonder if she's going to say something that'll drop me in it – if now is the time when my carefully constructed disguise is exposed. But then she spins on her heel and looks out the window, pointing to the car park.

'Maddy, look – that gorgeous supply teacher's back.' She pulls out her phone. 'Have we got science this morning? I can't remember this new timetable.'

Maddy, distracted, looks over her shoulder at the timetable on the screen. One of them whispers something and there's a stifled giggle. I make my escape.

*

'You OK?'

I sit down at the edge of the table in the common room that is reserved for the people who don't fit in. Allie's there, her hair piled up in a scruffy knot on top of her head, with strands hanging down over her ears to cover a sparkling row of piercings, which are definitely not allowed.

'Have you started reading the set text for English yet?'

She puts her chin in her hand and looks at me directly.

I shake my head.

'It's quite good, actually,' she continues.

I smile with my mouth closed. I can't think what to say. I think I've been a social outcast for so long that I've forgotten how to do conversation.

'All right?' Rio gives me a nod and sits on the edge of the table opposite me. His hair is bleached pale at the tips and spikes up. The back's been shaved. There's a strict rule about hair dye at school, and I'm not sure how he's got away with it.

'You did it, then?' Allie reaches out and runs a hand across the spiky ends of his hair.

'Yes – but I'm in the dog house because I've messed up the eco balance of the septic tank or something.'

'With what?'

'Bleach.'

'That'll do it.' Allie came to the school from Birmingham a few years back, and her accent hasn't softened at all. She offers me a piece of chewing gum.

'Thanks.'

'Isn't Mrs Lennox going to go mad when she sees

it?' I find myself asking him.

'Hair must be a natural shade, the rulebook says.' Rio grins. 'Blond is a natural shade. Just not mine.'

Allie laughs. 'I reckon they don't notice us anyway.'

I flick a glance at her and Rio. They both stand out because they don't appear to give a shit. But they're still sitting here with me in the social-reject corner, not hanging out with Lauren's friends or even the premier-league gang. They're the pinnacle of social achievement around here – and Madison is desperate to be part of it. Lauren – before she sort of stepped away from me – used to tell me all about it. Madison spends all her spare time checking up on Kira Matheson and her little Queen Bee collective.

School is a complicated social structure. I think sometimes it's easier being one of the rocks that orbits the planet, minding my own business. It's just a bit lonely sometimes.

I spend all day half expecting Lauren to track me down to find out what's happening. It's the strange thing about families like ours: we *were* one; then we weren't any more. But you can't just turn it off like that. I get the feeling she knows something is up.

There must be loads of families like ours, where the kids are left trailing after the adults, suddenly expected to start a new life with new parents. Meanwhile the little box room that used to be hers still has the stickers she stuck along the edge of the cabin bed Neil made for her when they moved in. And took down again when they moved out, when he met Clare at work and dumped Mum and me for a new life.

So when I walk home from school (on my own, to our house at the top of the town on the very last row of houses on the estate), I don't know why, but it's not really a surprise when I get back to Miller Terrace and Lauren's sitting on the wall outside our house. She's carried on visiting ever since Neil and Mum split up, but when she does I always tend to stay out of the way because I feel like I want her to have space. Maybe it comes across as being a bit stand-offish, but I don't want to intrude. And she gets on well with Mum.

I know I shouldn't, but I sometimes resent the fact that when she turns up, somehow Mum manages to gather herself and be lovely and warm and bright. I know it's just because she can do it in small bursts, but sometimes I wish she'd fake it for me too. I don't always want to see the reality of the way she feels. So I just disappear to my room when Lauren turns up, but this time it's a bit different.

'I was just—'

'Passing?'

Lauren flashes a smile at me for a second – and it's genuine – and she pushes me with her foot, teasing, so her bag drops down on to the pavement. I pick it up without thinking.

'Watch the property,' Lauren says, snatching it out of my hand with a laugh.

'Sorry,' I say, in a voice that tells her I'm not.

It's an expensive one – proper leather – probably from somewhere in Edinburgh. Mine came from Falkirk Market, and where it's scuffed you can see the weave of fabric beneath the fake black leather stuff. I feel a bit ashamed of it and turn it round quickly so the scuffed bit doesn't show. You get good at that sort of thing when you don't have much money. It's almost like a habit. I've got excuses ready in case people want me to go places (that one makes me laugh . . . nobody ever asks me to go anywhere), and I can make one drink last ages in Burger King.

'Are you going to let me in, then, or what?'

Lauren jumps down from the wall and stands by the front door. I feel the familiar lurch of anxiety knowing what's inside. Even though she knows what the house is like, there's something about opening the door – it's like admitting it to myself all over again.

I try the handle. It's not locked. 'You could've just gone in.'

'I didn't like to.' Lauren twists her mouth, biting the inside of her cheek the way she's always done when she's anxious.

'Holls?' Mum's voice comes from the sitting room.

The front door slams back against the wall and rebounds, hitting me in the face.

It takes a second before I realize why. I've been so used to pushing hard against the sea of crap that has silted up the hall that when the door meets – nothing – it swings back hard. The force has to go somewhere.

I look behind it, at the space at the bottom of the stairs

where the boxes and bags and piles of unopened letters and black bags full of too-small clothes that are destined for the charity shop but have sat there forever should be and . . . there's nothing. Just the carpet, which looks oddly bare.

And – I realize – the smell isn't the same. It smells of something vanilla-ish and sweet, like –

'Well, hello.'

Cressi opens the kitchen door.

'You've brought a friend home,' she says, looking happy. 'I'll put the kettle on, shall I? Or do you want some toast? Young people always like toast.'

I shake my head, catching Lauren's eye and laughing.

'This isn't a friend . . .' I stop, realizing what it sounds like. 'It's . . . This is Lauren.'

'Aha.' Cressi smiles broadly. 'The mysterious stepdaughter. I was beginning to think they'd made you up.'

I point to a framed photograph on the wall of the two of us, soaking wet in swimsuits, laughing in the garden. I remember that summer day so clearly.

'Never noticed that before,' says Cressi. 'Hopelessly unobservant, that's me. Anyway, can I feed you two chaps?'

'I don't think there's any bread,' I say.

'Oh, there is,' Cressi says. 'I've done a supermarket run.'

There's a crashing noise from the sitting room. Lauren looks quizzical, but I shake my head and roll my eyes as if to say *don't worry*. I'm getting used to the sound of Mum's battles with her crutches.

'Do NOT move,' Cressi booms in the direction of the door. She points to the space under the stairs. 'Put your bags there and hang up your blazers. I've just tidied; I don't want this place piled up with teenager rubbish.'

There's a space under the stairs. It takes a second for me to register this fact.

Lauren follows me into the sitting room. It's – tidy. There's a bunch of bright pink carnations in a vase on the coffee table and the carpet's been hoovered. The television is on mute, and behind a newly shining screen a newsreader mouths silently. All the books on the shelves have been lined up neatly, and the windowsill is clear and sparkling clean. The whole room smells of furniture polish. And Mum is sitting there on the chair, crutches crossed on the floor in front of her (that's what the crash was a moment ago) and a heap of cushions behind her back. Her leg is propped up on two pillows.

'Oh my God,' Lauren says, looking down at Mum. 'Are you OK? What's happened?' She turns to me and frowns. 'Why didn't you tell me?'

'I tried,' I mutter, but I think back. I don't know how to say I wanted to tell her, but her friends are terrifying.

'Do you like my new cast?' Mum leans forward and pats it. It's red and made of rough, hard, plastic stuff.

She reaches across, taking my hand and giving it a squeeze.

Lauren squats down on the other side of the sofa beside Mum, who puts an arm round her waist and pulls her close for a kiss.

'Hello, darling – how are you?'

Lauren pulls a face. 'Surviving.'

She steps back and sits down on the edge of the no-longer-crap-strewn coffee table. For once I don't feel ashamed of the state of the place. And Mum, despite her broken ankle, looks quite happy sitting there.

'Tea?' I stand up, thinking maybe I'll give them time to talk.

'Can I have juice, please?' Lauren asks.

'Course.' I assume there is some, now the fridge has been filled by Cressi.

'So what's happening?' I take the milk out of the fridge and pass it to Cressi, who is shaking the teapot from side to side.

'Well, we've got the fibreglass cast on, so it's safe for her to be up and about – so that's a start. And I've had a go at the downstairs of the house.' Cressi indicates her car, and I realize it's stuffed full of black bin bags.

'Thank you.' My voice is gruff. It's a bit awkward.

'It's fine.' She plonks the tea in mugs on a tray and tips a packet of ginger snaps on to a plate, and we head back through.

I remember the juice for Lauren and turn back, hoping there is some in the fridge.

There's more than that. It looks like an advert. The shelves are packed with cheese and ham and big packs of ready-to-cook meals. There's milk and orange juice in the door, and the salad drawer's full of brightly coloured fruit and veg. And the dried-out old lemon is nowhere to be seen. I realize it must have cost a fortune, and I need to tell Cressi we'll pay her back. I'm not sure how, mind you.

I pour a glass of orange juice for Lauren and take it through to the next room.

It's so weird. I'd forgotten that there was so much light and space in the house. I mean, it's always going to be tiny – but we've been living under a mountain of Stuff for so long that now, with the downstairs cleared, it feels like a massive weight has been lifted. And the weird feeling I've got takes a moment to make sense. The whole place feels bright and clear and – I realize as I walk into the sitting room and hear Mum actually laughing with Lauren – *happy*. Like someone's shifted something besides bags and boxes. I feel like it's a home, not just a place I live. Somewhere I could imagine people coming inside.

'How was school?' Mum reaches out to me again, lacing her fingers through mine.

'Fine,' I say.

'Cressi's taken over.' She raises an eyebrow, the one with the hoop through it.

'I can see that.' I smile back at her.

'I'll have a go at the upstairs tomorrow,' Cressi says, taking a sip of tea.

Mum stiffens slightly in her chair. 'It's fine, honestly. I really appreciate it, Cressi, but we can sort it out.'

I dart a look at Lauren.

'Don't argue.' Cressi's tone is firm. 'I won't sell or recycle or chuck anything without your express permission.'

And I hold my breath for a second. I've seen the way Mum reacts when Neil turns up here and makes a comment about the state of the house. I know how proud she is – too proud to accept help until now – and how ashamed. And I half expect her to fight back.

But she doesn't.

'Fine.' She sits back against the cushions and shifts her new red cast slightly.

I take a breath and look around the room. Lauren sips her juice.

'It just needed a bit of a sort-out.'

'Well,' says Mum, shuffling on the seat and pushing a cushion down behind her back, 'I really appreciate it.'

'You'd do the same for me.'

Mum pulls a face. 'I'm not sure you'd thank me for it. I'd disorganize all your neatly ironed tea towels, for one thing.'

Lauren looks at me over the top of her glass. She doesn't know Cressi or how gorgeous and magazine-perfect her house is.

Even before our house spiralled downwards into the chaos we've been living in, Mum wasn't ever exactly tidy. It was a sort of happy jumble of books and pets and baking. Before she had me, she was in a band, so the house was hung with posters and black-and-white photos of her with friends she knew when she used to have a life. My words, not hers.

'How's your dad?'

Mum's voice breaks through my thoughts. Her tone is

careful, the way it always is when she asks Lauren that question.

Lauren rolls her eyes. 'He's going on holiday to Barbados with Clare next month, so he's fine.'

'What about you?'

'Oh, I'm not invited.'

I watch Mum's nostrils flaring. Her lips are pressed together. She doesn't say anything for a moment.

'You're not staying at home alone?'

Lauren shakes her head. 'Clare's sister is coming to stay, apparently.'

'And who's Clare's sister when she's at home?'

'Emma.' Lauren's voice is flat.

There's an awkward silence. I know Mum is trying to think of the right thing to say, and I feel bad that even though my life here isn't full of expensive leather bags and designer trainers like Lauren wears, I don't feel like a spare part.

I run my hands along the pink frilly stuff that edges the sofa. The chairs were my granny's, and the velvet material has faded to a pale dusky pink. But if you lift up the material where it gathers around the buttons, you can see the original dark pink it used to be years ago. Lauren and I used to make dens out of the cushions, stacking them up along the top and pushing the sofa out from the wall. We'd put a blanket on the floor, and Mum would make us a picnic lunch, and we'd pretend we were camping. I look at her, sitting on the edge of the coffee table, her hands wrapped round the glass, and I wonder if she remembers.

'I'm sure it'll be fine,' Lauren says, putting down the glass and standing up.

It's funny, but you can actually watch the veneer covering over the cracks as she stands there. She pulls her hair over one shoulder, smoothing it with a hand and checking her reflection in the mirror. With a finger, she dabs at the pale pink lipstick she's applied on the way out of the school gates – which is still perfect, and doesn't need fixing – and pushes her shoulders back.

'I'd better be going, anyway. Just thought I'd come and say hello and see how you were doing.'

'You don't need a reason,' says Mum, smiling again. 'You're welcome any time, darling. You know that.'

Lauren gives a nod, but her lips are set in a tight little smile. I know – because no matter how much she wishes I couldn't, I can tell what she's thinking – that she's upset. And I also know that an upset Lauren is most likely to lash out with vicious words, and I feel myself bracing, instinctively.

But she doesn't.

She hooks her bag over her shoulder and heads out of the room.

'I'll see you later,' she says, and doesn't turn back as she walks out, so she misses the kiss that Mum blows at her, and then the little sad smile that lifts her face for a moment, then passes.

'Right, then.' Cressi stands up. 'I'd better be off too. No rest for the wicked.'

'Are you working tonight?' Mum asks.

It's already quarter to five.

She shakes her head. 'No, but the dogs have been in all afternoon, and Phil's back from work later.'

She picks up my cup and Mum's from the coffee table, and goes through to the kitchen. A couple of moments later, there's the sound of running water as she fills the washing-up bowl.

'We've been organized,' says Mum, and she gives me a smile.

I look down at the red stuff on her leg and place my hand on it – carefully, because I don't know if it's sore.

'It doesn't feel like I expected.'

'It's a lot lighter than the plaster one they put on. Apparently that's called a back slab, and it was just to hold it in place until this one.'

'Can you walk with it?'

'Only on crutches. Apparently it'll be five weeks before they take this off – and only then if the X-ray is *satisfactory*.' The word has invisible quote marks around it.

'And –'

'So –'

We both laugh.

Mum gives a nod of her head. 'You first.'

'So what happens now?'

It's strange, but I feel like everything's shifted slightly – with the new clean space all around us, there's a weird feeling, like Mum doesn't quite know what to do with herself.

'Well, Cressi's doing the dishes, then I assume you're going to the pool, and then apparently we're having macaroni cheese for dinner.'

'The pool's tomorrow.'

I feel my stomach do a cartwheel as I say the words. And I swear my cheeks have just gone pink, and I really, really do not want to have That Conversation right now. But the promise of tomorrow fizzes inside me, like the best kind of secret.

'OK – well, in that case, you've probably got homework?'

'Not really.' I find myself thinking about the pool, and my stomach gives a whirl of excitement when I think of the boy at the bus stop. That all seems like a million years ago.

'So what are you doing now?'

I look at Mum sideways. It's as if she's had a bump to the head when she fell and broke her ankle. For the last few years, she's been in some sort of daze, apparently oblivious to stuff like parents' evenings and homework assignments. I've had to chase myself to get them done, knowing that they weren't going to do themselves and also that I didn't want to completely screw everything up. I realize that she's become so inward-looking that she hasn't a clue what I do with my time.

'Maybe you could get started on tomorrow's homework?'

I've been the grown-up in this house from the moment I became a teenager. And now, somehow, with a broken ankle, my mother has decided to take over again.

It feels weird.

CHAPTER EIGHT

So I'm on my way to the pool. Cressi offered me a lift, but I made an excuse because I wanted to land at the bus stop and not straight at the leisure centre, just in case. I know it's ridiculous to think that he might be there, but I can't help imagining it anyway.

And I'm telling myself that he won't be there, because that way I don't have to feel disappointed . . . but I'm also thinking if he isn't, I don't have to worry about the fact that I'm still wearing my slightly-too-small swimsuit under my clothes and that, despite the fact that we've got a box with twenty-four pairs of goggles (late-night QVC order last March), we've got no money to buy me a new one. And I used my last money on the taxi to and from the hospital, so I now have no data left on my phone.

'Hey.'

I scramble off the bus and WHAM, just like that, he's there. That wasn't even on my list of potential things that might just happen. And it's the weirdest thing because my knees just go ZING and my stomach does this flipping-over thing and I feel like there is no escaping the fact that I really fancy this boy. He's not like the boys at school who are either geeky or cocky and smart-arsed and think they're all that. He's different. He's got a sort of aura around him. And I know. I know, I sound like a complete loser. But you know what? I kind of feel like I'm owed something nice like this. And I let myself smile at him, not looking down and feeling like I have to stoop like I do at school where everyone is about a foot smaller than me and I feel like a giant.

'What are you doing here?'

He gives a sort of half smile. 'What's a nice boy like me doing in a bus stop like this?'

'Something like that.' I don't even know who I am. Am I flirting?

'Well, I've been sitting here since the other day waiting for you to come back. I'm bloody glad I only had to wait three days. I thought you might only come once a week.'

And he laughs.

This is not my life.

I like his big mouth and his strong eyebrows and the fact that he is possibly the most comfortable-in-his-own-skin person I've ever met.

'Well, you're lucky I happen to be working this evening,' I say, and I start walking.

He falls into step beside me, and we walk up towards the pool.

'So we have yet to be formally introduced.'

'This is true,' I say.

He swings round, holding out his hand.

I shake it, laughing – and I feel a fizzing of electricity that shoots down my arm and all the way through my body and to the very end of my toes – and we stand for a second.

'Edward Jarvis.'

Edward. Not only does he sound posh, he has a posh name.

'Ed for short. Unless you're my mother, in which case . . .' He shakes his head and pulls a face, his mouth turning down at the corners.

'Holly Gilmour.'

He shakes my hand (which he is still holding, for which I have no words that would make sense) once more, and then releases it and bobs his head. 'How d'you do.'

He really is posh. I've never heard anyone say that in real life before.

'We'd better get a move on. Don't want you to be late for work.'

'So – you going swimming too?'

'I thought I might, yes.'

I hadn't noticed until now, but he's got a sports bag slung over one shoulder and the same hoody that's a bit short on the sleeves. And the little hole in the toe of his trainers is a bigger hole now. It makes me feel better about my crappy clothes.

We walk up the steps towards the pool, and I notice there's a gang of kids – presumably from the high school – hovering outside the door.

I brace myself. In Kilmuir, this would mean a load of hassle, some sarcastic comments about my hair or my height or my clothes . . . but, here, I just walk in, and it's not until we're standing in the reception area and the air is heavy with the smell of chlorine that I notice they're peering through the glass and looking at us.

'Do you know them?'

I look at Ed, who has pulled out his phone. He's not actually doing anything on it – he just opens it, swipes at the screen and then clicks the home button so it closes again. He shoots a quick glance outside at the window.

'Nah.'

But I recognize that look. I sense the feeling that he's glad he's made it through there without getting a mouthful of abuse about something. But I don't say anything – I don't want to spoil things. Years of being at the bottom of the heap has meant I've learned self-preservation methods – the tactical road-crossing and phone-checking, shoelace-tying and sudden mime performance of *oops, I forgot something really important* for a non-existent audience. Ed's doing the same thing here. I wonder if he's in the same social strata as me, but I can't see how he can be when he's so casually posh and sort of comfortable with himself.

'What time do you call this?'

Cressi's sergeant-major bark echoes across the foyer. I look across and see her striding back from the office, a pair of terrifying turquoise Crocs on her feet.

I look up instinctively at the clock on the wall. I didn't think we were late and –

'Joking.' Cressi laughs. 'Aha – I see you've brought your plus one. Are you a new recruit?'

Ed points a finger to his chest in a *Who – me?* gesture.

'Yep – you.' She marches across to us, pulling out the band from her frizzy bun as she does so and yanking it back into submission. A few rebellious strands fuzz out immediately, so her head retains its halo of curls.

'This is my –' I stumble over the word 'friend' because I realize it sounds a bit presumptuous when we've only had two short conversations. 'Edward.'

As I'm cringing at the fact I've just implied he's 'my Edward', Cressi has already taken charge.

'How d'you do, Edward.'

Second time I've heard that in the space of an hour. I feel like I've moved to another planet. She gives him a sergeant-major handshake.

'Sorry to steal Holly away from you, but we've got a full class today, and the twins from hell are back from their trip to Malaga, so I'm going to need all hands on deck ASAP.'

'I'll see you—' I begin, but Cressi has taken me by the arm and is propelling me in the direction of the changing room. I can already hear the blood-curdling shrieks of the terror twins and their harassed mother, Jennifer. This is going to be the longest half hour of my week.

I roll my clothes in a ball and shove them into the top of my bag, clicking the locker shut. This is the first time I've worn the official swim-instructor volunteer kit – shorts and a black polo shirt over my swimsuit, my hair tied back in a ponytail. The logo looks very official.

'Now, boys,' I hear the twins' mother saying, one held firmly by the hand, the other trying to soak his head under the drinking fountain. 'You've got a new teacher today. Look – there she is.'

She points to me, and the smaller of the two sticks his tongue out at me before flashing a gap-toothed grin.

'You look very impressive,' says a voice behind me.

It's Ed, unselfconscious in his swimming trunks. He pulls his goggles down over his head, and just as I'm about to say something – or think of something to say – one of the twins pipes up.

'Is that your boyfriend?'

'Shh, boys,' says their mother. Her hair – damp from the heat of the pool – is falling in her eyes, and she swipes a lock of it back behind her ear.

'Why don't you two come and sit over here on the side with me and wait for the others,' I say, and my voice sounds a lot firmer than it feels.

The mum gives me a look of such gratitude that I feel sorry for her. At least she's getting half an hour off now, even if she's got to sit in the tiny, crowded spectator section with the rest of the baking-hot, totally harassed swimming-lesson parents.

'Can we get in now?'

Demon twin #1 – the gap-toothed one – gets up from the ledge where they're supposed to sit and wait, and darts towards the edge of the shallow end.

'No!' I say, and I raise a finger in warning. 'Sit down there right now, or you'll be on the side for the whole lesson.'

There's a split second when I think Oh God, he's going to burst into tears, but then he shuffles his bum back on the ledge so he's leaning against the wall and crosses his arms, looking mutinous.

'Excellent work,' says Cressi from behind me. 'I can see you're going to be a natural at this.'

And it turns out that I love it. I know Cressi, so I realize her bark is far sharper and more terrifying than her bite, but the children don't – so they're on their best behaviour. She's kind and funny, with a sense of humour so dry that it goes right over the head of most of the children in the lessons, and a good number of the parents too. We have the tiny ones holding on to floats and kicking, and I manage to get Amelia ('Tears before bedtime, that one,' Cressi says under her breath to me as she approaches for the five o'clock lesson) to let go of the side of the pool and try floating on her back.

I'm concentrating so hard that I even forget that Ed's in the pool – until, that is, Cressi nudges me and points to him as he powers down the fast lane, arms slicing through the water effortlessly.

'You didn't tell me your friend Edward was a pro.'

We watch as he hits the end, disappears for a few seconds as he executes a perfect tumble turn, and emerges halfway down the pool.

'I didn't know.'

I realize afterwards, as I'm rubbing my hair dry with a towel, that he might still be swimming. It's not like we made any arrangements to meet up afterwards, or anything, but . . . I have a look around the changing room and realize he's half leaning, one leg crossed over the other, by the side of the lockers.

He looks up from his phone and smiles. 'Are you done?'

'I am,' I say. 'I was just looking for you.'

A dimple flickers in his cheek when I say that, and I realize in that second that maybe – just maybe – he's not as super confident as he appears to be.

'And here I am.'

'And here you are.'

'It's boiling. Shall we go and get a drink or something?'

I nod.

Cressi is in the foyer as we open the door from the changing rooms, and the cool air hits me in the face.

'See you later, Holls,' she says. And she looks at Ed for a second. 'Pretty impressive swimming there, young man.'

Ed ducks his head. 'Thanks.'

I walk along the high street with Edward, heading for the pound shop. It's the strangest feeling being here. We're only three miles from home, and it's familiar – we've been coming here since I can remember to catch the train into Edinburgh and to go to the little book shop. But, at the same time as it's familiar, it reminds me of the feeling of being on holiday – I can let my guard down, because I don't have to worry that someone from school's going to turn up and start taking the piss out of my clothes or my general existence.

Despite earlier, Ed seems quite relaxed too. We grab drinks and a packet of Oreos from the shop – I offer him a pound, but he shakes his head.

'It's fine,' he says. 'You can get them next time.'

As we walk out of the shop, I catch a glimpse of myself in the glass of the door. There's a smile I can't hide at the thought of there being a 'next time'.

It's still really hot, even though it's late – almost seven – and the shadows are lengthening. We walk down the stonewalled path to the canal and sit by the water's edge on one of the wooden picnic benches, facing each other. The sunlight flashes and dapples on the canal, reflecting the sky and the branches of the willow trees that hang down, reaching as if they're trailing their fingers in the water. The bench smells of hot-baked wood, and I run my fingers across it, feeling the grain, which has been smoothed out after years of weathering. It's one of my favourite places to sit, but normally I'm here alone.

'I'd better just text my mum,' I say, realizing as I do that I sound about twelve. I pull my phone out of my jeans pocket and remember there's no credit on it. I'll have to use the borrow-a-quid thing.

'Me too.' Ed mirrors my movements, and as we're both typing he looks up for a second at the same time as I do, and he catches my eye.

'She worries,' he explains.

'Mine does too.'

'I keep trying to point out that I'm six foot one and hardly likely to be abducted, but she's convinced that every time I go out someone's going to try and lure me away to see their puppies.'

'Mine has a broken ankle.' I don't add that, actually, it's not really her that worries – although she does, just not about things like that – it's me. I've sent a text saying *Just out of swimming. Won't be long. Is everything OK?* and I'm trying to remind myself that she's probably just drinking tea and her phone's out of reach.

I put my phone back in my pocket and pull open the packet of Oreos, extract one, and begin to dismantle it, twisting it round so it splits in two. I am about to lick the filling off the biscuit when I realize that maybe that's a bit gross, but –

'That's how I eat them too.' Ed reaches across to the packet, grabs a biscuit and twists it apart.

He raises his eyebrows at me.

'Terrible manners,' he says, laughing as he hands me the other half of his cookie.

Together, sitting by the water as the ducks splash and potter in the canal, and the willow branches sway in the breeze, we deconstruct all the cookies, and talk, and it's strangely not uncomfortable.

'How come Cressida is so posh?'

It's my turn to raise my eyebrows. Ed's accent is not exactly the usual for round here.

'How come you can tell she's posh when you're so posh yourself?'

'I'm not. I just went to school in Edinburgh. Everyone there sounded the same. I think it's because half the parents are English.'

He says all that in his posh accent, which makes me

want to laugh, but then I think about the boys hanging around outside the pool and how Allie gets picked on for sounding weird, and I realize that maybe he doesn't need to be reminded of that.

'Cress is English,' I explain. 'She moved up here when her husband got a job transfer. He's in the army or something, I think.'

She's sort of comfortably terrifying. If you were in trouble, I get the feeling that Cress would sort it out in no time, in her no-nonsense, efficient sort of way. Then afterwards she'd bollock you for being an idiot, and you'd try harder next time. If all teachers were like her, I think school would be bearable. Almost.

'That explains the sergeant-major effect.' Ed grins.

His teeth are white and straight, and I wonder if he's had a brace. Mine are almost straight, but my front teeth cross over a little bit. Not enough to justify a brace, the dentist said, but enough that I notice perfect teeth in other people.

I want to ask him about that, and everything.

'Why don't you teach at the pool in Kilmuir?'

I glance away for a second and then fiddle with the friendship bracelet on my wrist, spinning it round. 'I just . . .'

'S'alright,' says Ed. 'I just wondered.'

'No, it's just . . . it's a bit like living in a goldfish bowl, and it's nice to escape sometimes.'

He nods, his mouth turning down at the edges, his face thoughtful. 'Yeah. That's why I like swimming.'

'Me too.'

'When you're in there, counting breaths, thinking about your strokes, there's no room to think about all the other shit.'

There's a second where his face is unreadable and he looks blank, before he shakes his head.

'Sorry – don't mean to go all deep and meaningful on you.'

'I know what you mean.'

There's a moment where neither of us says anything, and we both look out at the canal. It's a bit awkward – well, it feels it to me, anyway, because I don't really make a habit of talking about how I feel about stuff. But it's strange and nice that he feels the same way about swimming as I do. Cressi has spent years trying to persuade me to join the team, but it's not about other people for me – it's the opposite.

'D'you want another? I'm always starving after swimming.' Ed pushes the Oreo packet across the table and three of them roll away like chocolate wheels. He reaches out and catches them, handing two to me and twisting the third apart and eating it.

My phone buzzes in my pocket and I pull it out.

Don't rush back if you're having fun.

Mum always says that. The thing is, I always do, anyway, because I'm worried that she's not OK.

I watch as a raft of ducks swims past – teenage, half-grown ducklings following their parents – and I remember a time when I didn't worry all the time about what my mum was doing.

'Everything OK?' Ed says, apparently noticing my distraction.

I nod, and we both reach for a biscuit at the same time so our hands touch. There's a feeling in my stomach like I just swooped underwater for a second, and I feel a catch in my breath. Ed cocks his head to one side and takes the Oreo from the packet.

He twists it apart and lays both halves on his upturned palm, stretching it out towards me.

'We can share it.'

The corners of his eyes crinkle up when he smiles. He rakes a hand through his hair, which has dried now and is flopping, dark and wavy, over his forehead.

I have never felt like this while eating a cookie. That's a sentence, I think to myself, that I never thought I'd hear.

Ed shoves the whole biscuit in his mouth sideways on, then puts a hand over his mouth. 'God, sorry,' he says, pulling a mock-horrified face. He takes his hand away.

'You've got –' I motion to my own face, quoting the packaging – '*delicious vanilla-flavoured filling* on you.'

'Where?'

'On your nose.'

'Where on my nose?' Ed's laughing as he leans forward across the table towards me.

'Here,' I say, tapping the left side of my nose with my finger. He brushes at the right side of his, as if we were mirror images.

'No,' I say, and I reach across and brush it off with a

finger, and I can feel my cheeks going scarlet. 'There.'

His eyes meet mine for a second, and the same feeling of swooping underwater hits me right in the depths of my stomach. I look away towards the canal, and there's a sudden flurry as a tiny moorhen dives under the surface in a rainbow of splashes hit by sunlight.

Ed's phone buzzes, and he pulls it out of his pocket. It's the third time in the last ten minutes, but he's been ignoring it until now.

'Shit,' he says, looking at the screen. 'I'm going to have to go.'

'You OK?'

'Yeah.' He shoves his phone back in his pocket after tapping a quick reply. 'It's just . . . It's nothing really.'

I pick up my bag and push the strand of hair that always comes loose from my ponytail back behind my ear.

Ed picks up the Oreo packet and crushes it in his hand, tossing it into the bin as we walk past and back up the lane to the high street. He's biting his lip and frowning. His stride is long – I manage to keep up, but we're walking fast, as if he's late for something. I check my phone for the time, realizing that I've just missed the bus and there's probably not another one for half an hour.

As we emerge from the gloom of the tree-shaded lane and through the passageway between the shops, a small red car hurtles to a stop in front of us. The side door is flung open.

'Where the bloody hell have you been?'

I can't see inside because the long shadows cast the

person in the driver's seat into darkness, but they are clearly Not Impressed. Ed leans down and folds the front seat forward. He throws his bag in the back seat and turns to look at me, an awkward expression on his face.

'Sorry, my mum – she's a bit—'

'Edward.' The voice from the car is flat and angry. I recognize that tone. Pissed-off parent is pretty much universal.

'It's fine – don't worry.' I look across the street and realize the bus must be late – it's turning round in the supermarket car park. If I run, I can make it.

'I wanted to . . .' He reaches into his back pocket, pulling out a blue Sharpie.

'We need to go,' says Ed's mum from the car. 'Now.'

'Give me your hand.'

He takes my left hand and scribbles his number on it. He shoves his hair back from his face again, and for a second the stressed-out look on his face is replaced with a smile.

'Just in case you've got any spare Oreos you want eaten.'

I let my hand drop down to my side as he folds himself into the impossibly tiny space in the front seat and slams the door shut. The little red car hurtles off, and it somehow looks as furious as his mother sounds.

CHAPTER NINE

When I walk into the common room the next day, Allie looks up, grins at me and shoves her chair sideways with a clatter of metal on tiles.

'All right?'

It's like clearing the crap in our house is making space for all sorts of things. The world feels brighter and less claustrophobic. I feel less invisible. Maybe it's because Cressi's filled the cupboards with food, and the washing's up to date, and my uniform smells of bluebell-and-lavender fabric conditioner ('Don't worry about the Tesco order,' she said when it all arrived at the door – there was tons of stuff, and it must have cost a fortune).

We sit and talk and laugh with Rio until the bell goes for form, and as we're leaving the common room, Allie says, 'D'you want to come out this evening? I'm going to Rio's place.'

I open my mouth to say no, I can't, I have to get back. But something stops me. And, in that second, I make a decision.

'Yes.' And I smile at her. A proper, open, let's-be-friends sort of smile. And the world seems to get a tiny bit bigger in that moment.

Allie lifts the metal bolt on the wooden gate that leads to Rio's house. We're in a meadow full of wildflowers, and as we walk I run my hands along the tops of the grasses, feeling them tickling my palms. It smells green and floral. Blue cornflowers are everywhere, and the whole place feels busy with bees and wildlife humming industriously. He told me at lunch that he can't stand living out here, but I think it's perfect. The path to the house is cut roughly with an old-fashioned hand mower, which is balancing against a pile of wood beside their cooking hut.

'Hello, you two.' A man with a grey-streaked beard appears. He's wearing a pair of faded old jeans, covered with rainbow splashes of paint, his curly hair sticking up untidily.

He cups a hand to his mouth, yelling in the direction of the field beyond. 'Ri!'

Rio walks out of the glass doors of their strange wooden house. It's shaped almost like an upside-down wooden boat, only with huge glass windows at the front. He's dressed in a new shirt, still creased in the lines where it's come out of the packet, and his hair is gelled into sharp, neat spikes.

'You look –' his dad's eyebrows lift momentarily – 'very dapper.'

'Thanks.' Rio shoots us a look that speaks volumes.

I'd be quite happy living out here. But Rio wants to live in the middle of the city in a sleek designer flat and get a job paying loads of money and have a convertible. He's working in the computer suite at school on some coding thing that's going to make him a millionaire. Apparently.

'This is Holly,' Rio says.

I half lift my hand and do a sort of awkward wave. 'Hi.'

Rio's dad smiles. 'Nice to meet you, Holly. I'll leave you three to it, shall I?'

And he disappears back inside, humming to himself. He looks exactly like you'd expect an artist to look.

As soon as he's gone, Rio turns to Allie.

'Did you get it?'

She reaches into her bag and pulls out a black aerosol can, throwing it to him.

'Oh my God, you are a star.' He catches it with one hand and spins it on his palm, beaming. 'Result.'

Rio unfastens the top two buttons of his new shirt and sprays copious amounts of Lynx over himself.

'Steady on,' says Allie, in a funny voice that makes us laugh. 'I thought we were taking Blue for a walk in the woods?'

Rio fastens up his shirt. 'We are.'

'So why are you . . . ?' Allie motions to his outfit and turns to me, pulling a face.

He looks like he's dressed to go into Edinburgh and spend the afternoon in a cool cafe, watching the world go by and sipping expensive cocktails.

'I happen to think it's important to dress the way you want to feel, Allie,' he says, teasing.

I look down at my faded T-shirt, jeans with a hole in the knee – and not the kind you buy in New Look – and beaten-up fake Converse. I'm clearly embracing tragic social outcast.

'Funny you should mention it.' Allie pulls open her plaid shirt, revealing a black T-shirt with *Hell Yes, I'm Gay* written on the front in red.

Clearly my gaydar is non-existent. I assume this means that, no, they're not a couple. At least that puts paid to the worries I was having as we walked here that I was going to end up feeling like a third wheel.

'Has your mother seen that?' Rio grins.

Allie nods her head.

'It's fine.' She rolls her eyes. 'She thinks it's ironic.'

'Still in her "it's just a phase" phase, then?'

'Deeply.'

Rio shoves the bottle of Lynx in his back pocket and looks over at Allie.

'You got anything to eat in that bag?'

She pats it, and it scrunches promisingly. 'Multipack of crisps.'

Allie's parents own the 7-Eleven shop on the edge of town. She explained on the way up that she's perfected the art of pilfering bits and pieces when they think she's helping out after school. So Rio, whose parents think that aerosol deodorant is an affront to mother nature, gets his Lynx fix once a fortnight when they get their delivery from the stockists.

I follow them as we walk in single file along the narrow path. The grass is long, and the silence is huge and fills my ears. We go beyond the field and climb over a gate.

Rio turns round. 'We're going to introduce you to The Clearing.'

They've got expectant looks on their faces, and I'm pretty sure my expression is a mixture of confusion and mild terror. We're in the middle of nowhere, and I don't actually know these people at all.

'Don't look so worried,' Allie says, laughing. 'It's a place, not some sort of satanic ritual.'

'Phew.'

'This way. It's not far.'

The branches are still wet from a rain shower earlier. As we scramble through the bushes, they slap us in the face – everything is green and lush. The sunlight shines through the leaves, dappling the still-damp earth.

We walk through some woods and into a space where the grass is jewel-bright. There's a makeshift tarpaulin canopy strung between two trees, some old pieces of cut logs, and a circle of biggish stones with a dark scar at its centre where a fire's clearly burned out sometime in the recent past.

With a yell, Allie takes a running jump at the tyre swing that hangs from the trees, throwing herself into the air. She startles a flock of birds from a nearby bush so they spiral upward, chattering in disapproval. She scuffs her feet on the ground, pushing herself up and up, flying above the dark green leaves of a rhododendron bush.

Rio bends down and pulls a mobile battery pack out of his bag.

There's a crackle of white noise, and then Oasis blares

out of the little Bluetooth speaker hung on a branch. When we were talking over lunch, it turned out that he's the only person I've met that has actually heard of Mum's old band, the Jade Stars.

'You free tomorrow night after school?'

Rio sits down on a log, fiddling with the cuffs on his shirt, and then brushing away an imaginary speck of dirt.

I don't know if he's talking to me or just to Allie, so I clear my throat and try to look as if I'm just very interested in the patch of clover by my feet. I bend down and pick a couple of leaves up.

'Dad's got some installation thing he wants to deliver to the gallery for someone. Apparently they're interested in buying a load of his stuff, so we can get a lift into town if you want?'

'Anything to get out of this hellhole,' says Allie, wriggling out of the tyre swing and tugging at the knot at the top of her rucksack to get the crisps. She rips the multipack open and throws us each a bag.

'What about you, Holly?'

'Oh – I –' I sort of wish I was free. 'I can't. I'm working at the pool.'

'Next time, maybe?' Rio says, through a mouthful of crisps. And I'm relieved, because I feel like I haven't missed my chance after all.

We talk and listen to music, and I take my turn on the tyre swing, pushing myself backwards and forwards, the toe of my shoe scuffing in the circle of dirt we'd worn underneath it. It feels nice to be part of something.

We walk home hours later, when the sky is streaked pale pink. I put in my headphones and listen to music as I make my way back up through town, and my stomach fizzes with nerves and excitement. I look at the faded number that's still just about legible on my hand, and I can feel Ed's hand holding mine as he scribbles it on there in his big, bold writing. I haven't texted him yet – not because I'm playing it cool, but because the thought of it is half exciting and half terrifying. It makes a shiver go right down my spine.

I get home and it takes the second between putting my hand on the door and it being opened from the inside just as I push it from the outside to make the connection: the shiny, incredibly posh-looking new car parked outside belongs to Neil.

'Holly, darlin',' he says, coming towards me in the tiny hall with his arms outstretched. It's so small and he's so big that he basically takes up all the space, but that's the sort of person he is. My ex-stepdad. My mum's ex-boyfriend. The man who used to live here but doesn't any more. I never quite know what I'm supposed to call him, so I tend to cycle between all of the above.

'Putting on the beef a bit there, aren't we?' he says, and he pokes my stomach.

There's a brief moment where – in my imagination – I punch him square in the not-inconsiderable gut, and while he's doubled over, I point out loudly that a) women come in sizes other than six to ten, and b) it's none of his (insert some swear words here) business. But that's only in my imagination. In reality, I find myself sucking my stomach in, catching a glimpse of myself in the hall mirror, realizing that it doesn't matter what I do, I'm never going to fit into his category of Acceptable Female Shapes, and, actually, I don't care.

'Lovely to see you too,' I say, realizing he won't even notice the sarcasm in my tone.

'I hear you've got yourself a little job at the pool?' He raises his eyebrows. 'That'll get the weight off, anyway. No need to be worrying about it.'

Lauren emerges from the kitchen with a pot of tea and four mugs on a tray and has the decency to look embarrassed – whether it's at his complete lack of tact or just the awkwardness of the situation, I don't know. I always wonder what it'd be like to be in a Disney-style family of two point four children and a dog, instead of this weird mismatched collection of people who float in and out of my life.

'I was just saying.' Neil's tone is injured.

'Dad,' she says, and gives him The Look.

'What?' he says, and winks at me. 'Holls knows I'm only kidding, don't you, darlin'?'

I give him a very fleeting thin-lipped smile. He puts his arm around my shoulders and squeezes. I stand completely still with my teeth gritted.

Seriously, Neil, stop talking.

I have literally no idea what my mother saw in him, and I have literally no idea why he and Lauren are somehow in my house, taking up my space, drinking our tea.

'Everything OK out there?'

Thank God Mum's on my side, even if she is pinned to the sofa.

'Coming,' I say, and I head into the sitting room where she's parked, her broken leg balanced on a cushion on the coffee table (still tidy, but then I suppose she's not in a state to make a mess when she can't move).

'You're late back,' she says, patting the space next to her. I sit down and she bobs her shoulder against mine like always.

'Yeah, I was hanging out with some friends . . .' I pause for a second, realizing that Lauren is sitting very still and listening to our conversation from the armchair by the television. 'Just some people from school.'

'Oh! That's lovely to hear, darling.'

I cringe at the very clear implication that I have no life, and try to give her a look that says *How long are they staying?* but it's not very easy to convey that many words in a glare. I'm aware that I'm flaring my nostrils and my eyes are popping, and Neil's giving me an odd look.

'You feeling OK, Holls?'

'Fine, thanks.'

There's a silence while Lauren pours out the tea and fetches a carton of milk from the kitchen. She doesn't bother with a jug.

Everyone has a drink and we all sit there, the clock on the wall ticking loudly.

'Anything good on the telly tonight?' asks Neil, and I can't help it – I glance over at him and back at Mum. Have

I missed something crucial? Have he and Lauren moved back in this afternoon?

'There's that David Attenborough thing,' says Mum, picking up the remote control.

'Oh God, they bore the arse off me.' Neil laughs slightly too loudly and stops when nobody else joins in. 'Still, Clare loves them. I reckon that'll be us this evening: bottle of red and a takeaway.'

Lauren looks pissed off. I know she doesn't really get on with Clare, and I suspect she's got better things to do at half eight on a Friday night than sit here making polite conversation with her sort-of-ex-family.

'We were waiting for you to get back, Holly,' Mum says, shifting herself in the chair so she can see me. Her leg scoots along the newly polished coffee table on its cushion, looking like one of the Queen's Crown Jewels on display.

'You were?'

'Neil's got a favour to ask. It's OK with me, but I thought I'd better run it past you.'

I look over at Lauren, who is picking at the pale pink varnish on her thumbnail. She doesn't look up at me.

'What is it?' I cup my mug of tea with both hands, holding it like a little beacon of warmth in front of me. Outside the sky is still the brightest blue and the barley field is turning from greenish to pale gold.

'Turns out Clare's sister Emma's not around the fortnight we're off to Barbados.'

'Nice,' I say in Lauren's direction, and I can hear a tiny hint of bitterness sneaking into my voice, and I don't like myself for it. 'Looks like you just scored a holiday after all.'

Lauren looks up at me for a moment, but she doesn't look triumphant. She looks uncomfortable, and a bit awkward.

'I said I'd have to check with you, but, if it was OK, Lauren could stay here.'

I look at Mum again. I can't convey anything to her via the silent staring method because Lauren is right in my eyeline. If I could, it would be along the lines of *Oh my God is this a joke you realize all her friends hate me and I'm going to feel uncomfortable the whole time she's here* . . . but then I see Lauren's mouth twisting sideways in that way it does when she's thinking about things or feeling uncomfortable, and I realize I can't say no. Which is, of course, exactly what Neil was banking on.

'That's fine,' I say airily. I don't add, *It's lucky the house has been completely blitzed from top to bottom by Cressi*, but I don't have to, because Neil does it for me.

'Course, I wouldn't have been asking if you hadn't got this place sorted . . . Between us, I was beginning to think you'd lost the plot completely.'

Lauren's eyes are circles of horror, and she looks at me for a second before turning to her father.

'Dad, you can't say something like that.'

Neil slurps down the last of his tea in a gulp. 'I speak as I find,' he says, giving a resonant belch.

Mum winces.

'Well, if that's sorted, I'd better hit the road,' he says,

picking up his keys and jingling them loudly. He does everything loudly.

Lauren gets up. She goes to put the mugs back on the tray – her tea is only half finished, as is mine and Mum's.

'Hang on, Neil – Lauren's not even finished.' Mum reaches out a hand.

'Time's money, darlin'.'

I catch Lauren's eye again, and she raises hers to the heavens for a brief moment. At least I only had to tolerate him for a few years. She's got him for life.

'Will you see them out?'

'Course.' I get up, leaving Mum on the sofa.

'See you soon,' says Neil, pinching my cheek like he used to when I was little.

Lauren hangs back for a moment as he's heading over to his Land Rover. She flicks a glance at me and pulls her long blonde hair into a ponytail in one hand, so she looks like she used to when we were at primary school, back when we were sisters.

'Thanks.'

I shrug. 'S'alright.'

I watch Neil inspecting the car for damage. He's parked it out of reach of the other cars, not realizing that the far end of the car park is where the kids from the estate all gather to play complicated games of tennis with made-up rules and nets made from strung-out cardigans. It's slap bang in the middle of a gaggle of children who are flailing rackets around and chucking balls in the air. He reverses out, narrowly missing a couple, and screeches off, Lauren in the passenger seat, her face blank.

With a sigh, I gather up the cups and wash them in the sink while Cressi's lasagne heats up in the microwave. The thing is, Neil can't be all bad, despite being a boorish, sexist, loud-mouthed, materialistic, thoughtless pig.

'Why?' I say, as I walk into the sitting room and flop down on the chair Lauren had been sitting in.

'Why are we having Lauren to stay while Neil and whatshername go on holiday?' (Mum always calls Clare 'whatshername'. I've given up correcting her.)

'No.' I swallow a mouthful of lasagne. 'Why on earth did you ever put up with him?'

Mum bursts out laughing. We've had this conversation before, approximately every single time he comes anywhere near us.

'Because I was young, and stupid – and because he looked like the sort of man who'd look after us.'

'Because he has a posh car?'

'He didn't then. He just seemed charming and nice, and he took me out for dinner, and I didn't have to think about everything.'

'But he's an arsehole.' I'm treading on dangerous ground here, because this might lead to a warning look and end of conversation . . . Not tonight.

'I know. He's stuck in some sort of 1970s time warp from the era that feminism forgot.'

'I feel sorry for Lauren.'

'I feel sorry for whatshername.'

I look at her sharply. 'You do?'

'God, yes.' Mum laughs. 'If he hadn't had an affair with her and waltzed off to live in her posh house, I might still be stuck with him.'

'You wouldn't, though,' I say, picking out pieces of onion and putting them to one side. 'You couldn't live with him.'

'I've lived with worse.' She looks at me for a moment.

I can't remember when she first told me the whole story.

When Mum was a teenager, her mum had a breakdown and was put into care. The place she lived in was so awful that she ran away as soon as she could, and found a crappy little bedsit above a sex shop in Camden. That's how she met the friends who became her first band, and that's why when she got pregnant and ended up back in Scotland, reunited with her mum, she was determined to make sure I never ended up in the same place. So she met Neil and tried to make it work. The longer she tried, the more affairs he had, and the more miserable she got. Eventually the affair with whatshername was the one that changed everything – because she was willing to provide him with what he wanted, which was basically a posh house, no mortgage and the chance to swan around on expensive holidays. Unfortunately with Lauren's mum dead, there was nowhere for her to go but along with him. That's why I can't really feel bad about her coming here.

I'd hate to be dumped like an unwanted pet every time something better appeared on the horizon, and that's exactly what Lauren's life seems to be. No amount of expensive designer stuff could make that OK. And, believe me, she has expensive designer stuff. Clare, aka whatshername, treats Lauren like a sort of living doll. She is the only person I know who has regular facials and manicures . . . admittedly my survey size is fairly small and consists of a) Cressi, who wouldn't have time for such nonsense, b) my mother, who still basically dresses like the 90s never ended, and whose idea of a hair treatment is a pot of gritty henna hair colouring from the health food shop and c) Allie, who, from what I know of her so far, is fiercely opposed to any kind of physical adornment, which she says is a tool of the patriarchy used to oppress us. In fact, the most high-maintenance person I know is Rio, but that's another story altogether.

I suppose there were times when we had fun with Neil. It's just you had to filter out the arsehole bits, and I can't work out if they're getting more frequent, or I'm just noticing them more.

'What's that on your hand?' Mum points to my left hand, where Ed's number is still scrawled in Sharpie.

'Just a number I needed to remember.'

She looks at me with her head cocked to one side, eyes narrowed. There's a pause. 'On your *left* hand?'

'Mm-hmm,' I say, casually, picking up the TV remote and switching over to the David Attenborough thing, which has already started. There's a zebra darting across the edge of a long stream, with a lion in pursuit. The water splashes up, slowing her down, and she stumbles for a second. I can't bear to watch.

'You're left-handed.'

I hit pause on the television and turn my eyes from the screen to look at Mum.

'I am. Ten out of ten for observation, Mother.'

'And you wrote this number you had to remember on your left hand?' She's laughing now. 'Anything you want to tell me about your after-swimming "chat with Cressida"?'

I half expect her to do bunny-ear air quotes round that bit.

'It was very nice,' I say, and turn back towards the television, picking up a cushion and hugging it in front of me, curling my legs up on the chair.

'I'm sure it was,' she says, and there's a tease in her tone. But she leaves it at that. She's always been the same — I think it's to do with having left home herself when she was so young, so she's never been as suffocating as some parents seem to be. She gives me more space to make my own mistakes than other parents do . . . but I've been so busy worrying about her for the last few years that I don't make any. It's as if the roles have been reversed, really. I check the post and give her the bills that need to be paid, remind her about school-trip letters, and make sure the washing's done, and that there's rabbit food, and bleach down the loo . . .

The zebra darts away from the water's edge and somehow confuses the lion, which keeps going for a second too long. The camera pans out, and we see the zebra galloping away to safety. There's probably a message in there, somewhere. I pass the remote control to Mum and head upstairs.

Hello.

I tap the words on my phone and look at them for a moment. Too formal and weird-looking.

Hi.

Capitals or no capitals?

hi!

Do I sound like a children's television presenter? I think I do. I'm perched on the edge of the bath watching the bubbles frothing up under the stream of the tap, and the mirror is steaming up. And I don't know what to say.

It's Holly.

I look at it for a moment. No, that looks even weirder, I think, but at the same moment my foot shoots out from underneath me because I'm balancing and the towel on the floor has slid on the lino, which is gleamingly spotless and shiny, thanks to Cressi. And there's a *zzzooomp* noise, because I've accidentally hit send.

Bloody hell.

Sorry, I didn't mean to send that.

I really need to get my act together. This is tragic.

I'm trying to compose a sensible third-time-lucky text, when a reply flashes up on the screen.

You're not Holly?

No, I am. I just meant I didn't mean to send that particular message.

Ah. I often send the wrong messages too.

Glad we've sorted that out! I type, and I feel my insides fizzing again. It's a weird feeling, but I don't want it to stop. Also, he's the only person I've ever known to type 'ah'

94

in a text message, which is more evidence of his poshness.

What're you up to?

I start to type *Running a bath*, but it makes me feel a bit shy, as if somehow Ed can see through the screen of the phone to me sitting here on the bathroom floor in a dressing gown.

Just reading, I reply. That's the sort of thing people do on a Friday night (if they've got no life, that is, which I guess there's no point trying to conceal).

Anything interesting?

Oh, brilliant. I turn the hot tap off and cast my eyes around the bathroom looking for inspiration.

Lord of the Flies, I write, with a flash of inspiration. It's been sitting on my bookshelf forever. I love reading, and I have literally no idea why I didn't just say that I'm re-reading *The Hunger Games* for the millionth time, or that I've borrowed so many new books from the library that I can't even remember the titles. Instead I've said that because it makes me sound clever and Ed's really posh.

Did you know that Stephen King uses Castle Rock as the town name for lots of his books? Another text follows straight afterwards: **You probably did. I'm showing my geek side, right?**

I didn't know that, I reply .

I don't know what Castle Rock is, and now I'm going to have to read the book to find out. I clamber up from the floor and head through to the bedroom with the phone in my hand. There's no reply. I feel a bit deflated and get into the bath with the book. Just as I set down my phone, it buzzes on the edge of the basin.

Are you doing anything on Sunday?

Ohhhhhh. I sit up in the bath and look at the phone.

Not really.

D'you want to come on a dog walk with me?

Just like that.

And my brain starts running at about a million miles an hour. Does he mean a dog walk, or a *dog walk*? What do you wear on a dog walk? I've got nothing except my black jeans, and I lent Allie my favourite T-shirt and –

Calm down, Holly. It's a dog walk.

OK, I type, and my stomach does something really weird and I feel tongue-tied all of a sudden like I don't know what to say, except I'm looking at a screen and not expected to say anything.

Excellent.

I look at the one-word reply and can't think what I'm supposed to say to that.

'Holly!' Cressi's voice calls up the stairs.

'I'm in the bath!'

'I'm not planning on joining you in there; I was just letting you know I've been in to check on Fiona. I've dropped off some shopping.'

She's like a foghorn. I can hear every word as clearly as if she was standing next to me. Thankfully she's not.

I look down at the phone again.

I'm trying to compose a reply when Ed beats me to it.

Meet you at the bus stop again?

OK, I message back. *When?*

Half one?

See you then.

I almost add, *I'll bring some Oreos*, but then I change my mind. It sounds a bit like I'm expecting something . . . like I feel like we've got some sort of shared thing in common. I look down at the blue numbers scrawled on my hand – his writing isn't tidy – and I realize that there's no way I'm going to get it off without scrubbing.

CHAPTER TEN

The back room that used to belong to Lauren has been tidied by Cressi, but there's still loads of my stuff on the shelves: boxes full of mementos from summers spent in England; old notebooks full of the stories I used to write in the holidays. I don't want Lauren's friends going through them and finding ammunition to make my life at school worse than it already is, so I'm clearing it properly before she moves in.

I can hear the clunk and shuffle of Mum on crutches, making her way from the sitting room through to the kitchen. She's getting a lot more mobile now she's used to them, and so far the house has stayed tidy. She seems much more like she used to be too – I don't know how long it'll last. She's been playing music when she hasn't for ages, and it's like she's waking up from hibernation.

'Do you want tea?'

'Can you make it one-handed?'

'I'm fine.'

She's learned to balance on one crutch and sort of shuffle from the kettle to the kitchen sink and back again.

I stack up a pile of old books and look at *Lord of the Flies*. For a second I contemplate doing a speed read so I sound like I know what I'm talking about. I shove it back on the shelf instead.

I trundle back and forth between the back room and my bookshelf, which is overflowing. One of the only advantages of Mum's obsession with cluttering up the house with random stuff over the last few years is that she's never said no to books . . . I think I've got more than most people I know (not that I know many).

'Tea!' Mum shouts.

She's sitting at the kitchen table in the little alcove bit of the kitchen. I pull out a chair and join her, reaching across and taking my favourite mug in my hands.

'It looks a bit weird, this place, doesn't it?' Mum motions to the tidy kitchen. The wooden shelves that Granny used to keep her ornaments on, which for the last few years have been stacked with random crap, are now empty.

'You mean organized?'

'Mmm.' She takes a sip of tea. 'I wanted to have a chat with you about that.'

I shift in my seat.

'Look, darling,' she says, and I realize that we're about to have One of Those Talks, and I feel a bit awkward. It's like she's woken up from being half asleep and realized the state of the place. 'I have been pretty crap, and I'm sorry.'

'You haven't.'

She looks at me and raises an eyebrow, pulling a face I haven't seen in years. 'I have.'

'You've not been well.'

'No.' She picks up a teaspoon and twirls it in her fingers,

looking thoughtful. 'I haven't. And to be honest I hadn't realized how unwell I'd been. But the house – and my leg—'

'It's OK.'

I twist the hem of my T-shirt, wrapping it round my finger and then spinning it out again so the fabric is all creased in the pattern of one of Mum's old tie-dye tops.

'When I went to the doctor the other day, we had a bit of a chat,' she carries on. 'And she asked me lots of questions, and I filled in some questionnaires and things.'

She puts the spoon down on the table and picks up her mug, looking down into it as if expecting to find the answers in there.

'We agreed that I've been in a bit of a muddle, and the main problem is that I have depression.'

I look around at the house and try to find the words to say, *Is that why we live in chaos?* But I don't think it would help.

'Do you think that's why we have all this –' I wave my hands around the tidy kitchen, motioning to the surfaces, which until last week had been choked with papers and washing baskets, books and boxes and things for a rainy day, Amazon orders that weren't even opened, and shopping-channel impulse purchases – 's-stuff?'

I stumble over the word. All these years – as the house has silted up with layers upon layers of things she's piled up and accumulated when she was working – the irony of her working online for a shopping channel isn't lost on me.

'I didn't buy it because I was saving it for a rainy day.'

Mum takes a sip of tea and looks at me directly. 'More like I bought it, then I didn't know what to do with it, and trying to work that out in my head made me feel even worse, so I just let it pile up.'

'So the house ended up being stacked up with stuff because you were depressed?'

'Basically.' She smiles at me, and she looks hopeful. 'I've arranged to see a counsellor for something called CBT, and apparently they're really good at helping you sort out your head.'

'I've heard of it. We talked about it in PSHE.'

'And I've got medication too.'

I'm still trying to get my head round the new improving-if-not-improved Mum. It all seems to have happened so fast. She shuffles on the chair and lifts up her cast to make it more comfortable on the cushion.

I allow myself a moment where I picture the house staying like this, and my old mum back: the one who used to sing and bake and grow herbs in the little pots outside the back door – the ones that are choked with dead weeds right now.

'That's the idea. We've been living like this for far too long, honey, and I want you to have your childhood back.'

I realize as she says this that she's got tears in her eyes. I climb out of the chair and kneel down on the floor and hug her round the middle, trying not to squish her cast as I do so. She smells warm and familiar, and she feels smaller. It's as if the last few years have made her shrink, but then I am six inches taller than her, I suppose. I'm six inches taller than everyone. Apart from Ed. I feel my cheeks stinging pink just thinking about him, and bury my face into the side of her cardigan.

'You're pretty bloody amazing, as kids go,' she says over the top of my head.

'I'm really not.' Inside, from out of nowhere, I feel a stab of resentment that Lauren's going to swan into our house just as everything is getting better and take up the whole space with her perfectness, and I'm going to be in the background being awkward and uncomfortable.

I feel like I spend my whole life thinking one thing and saying another and constantly juggling them, and I wonder for a moment if other people feel like that. And then I feel bad that I resent Lauren, because she's got her own crap to deal with.

'Well, we'll have to agree to differ on that one.' She drops a kiss on the top of my head, reminding me of being little. 'Deal?'

'OK.' I nod.

'Up you get,' she says. 'Your tea's going to go cold. What exactly is it you're doing upstairs, anyway?'

'Sorting out the box room for Lauren.'

'Oh, Holly.' She beams at me. It's been so long since she was this smiley that I'd forgotten what her face looks like when she's happy. My mum is actually really pretty. On the band poster that hangs in the hall, she's wearing her long hair down with daisies woven into it, and she's got a dress that looks like a nightie on and bare feet, and she's the one – there's always one person in a band, or in a group of friends – that everyone's eyes are drawn to. In that picture, it's Mum. I think it always was, but I don't think she ever really knew it. But whenever we go to England and see her old friends, they tell me how amazing she was and that they wish she'd join them or do something with her music.

The house has been so muffled with stuff and heavy with silence.

I get up to go and finish upstairs, and as I do I realize that Mum's flicked on the radio in the sitting room again.

When we were a family, the house was always full of music. From the moment we got up, it was on in the kitchen – and at night, when I went to sleep, I'd hear her downstairs, playing old CDs or her keyboard. It had been hidden under a pile of laundry for so long that I'd forgotten it existed, but it was polished and shiny now, under the window of the sitting room looking out over the fields. Maybe she'd start playing. Then I'd know she was really feeling better.

'You don't have to worry about making the bed,' her voice calls up the stairs.

I look down at the little single bed where Lauren's going to sleep and realize that Cressi's put fresh sheets on, and there's the faded flowery duvet cover on that used to be mine. It looks neat, but shabby. I feel a bit nervous at the idea of Lauren coming in, judging the way we live now. When she and Neil lived with us, we had more money, and the place didn't look so . . . battered. Even tidied up, it still looks nothing like her posh house. Just like I look nothing like her, with her expensive clothes and neatly cut hair. I catch a glimpse of my hair, which has dried after the bath into a tangle of red curls, and realize with a yawn I'm completely exhausted. This week feels like it's lasted a year.

CHAPTER ELEVEN

I feel so sick. It's not just nerves (but they are definitely not helping).

I'm on a bus, which is apparently being driven by a maniac, because we're hurtling round the bends on the narrow road to Hopetoun so fast that I'm jolting against the window. I check my phone again – it's quarter past one. At this rate, the ten minutes I was planning to spend at the bus stop gathering my thoughts and trying not to be nervous are going to be spent trying not to throw up on my shoes.

We sail over the hill into Hopetoun and slow down with a jerk as the sign saying thirty comes into view. I take a deep breath and look across the loch and the castle, watching the boats bobbing on the water as we judder to a halt at the first bus stop. We used to walk around there at the weekends, taking a picnic and dabbling our toes in the water. I watch a mum and dad and two little girls – one red-haired, one blonde, just like me and Lauren – as they set off along the path towards the woods. The bus pulls away, and I turn my head to try to see them again – but they've gone.

The high street is busy with the usual tourists – the castle brings visitors here from all over the world, partly because it was used as a film set in several different Hollywood movies. A group of American tourists flock to the bus as we stop outside the castle entrance. They're festooned with huge cameras and wearing brightly coloured raincoats, despite the sunshine.

'Does this go to Edin-boro?'

I smile to myself at the pronunciation, catching the eye of the old man sitting opposite. He raises his eyes to the sky and shakes his head in amusement.

'Afraid no'. This is for Kilmuir and Stonehouses.'

'Thanks so much,' says the tourist, and steps back.

I watch him pulling out a map and shaking it out as we drive on to the end of the street.

I can feel my heart thudding as the bus pulls to a standstill. It's a walk with a friend, that's all, I tell myself. I pull myself up, the metal of the rail cold against my hands, which are clammy with sweat and nerves. For a second I contemplate just sitting back down, letting the bus turn round, ducking out of sight as we head down the high street again. I could text Ed and tell him I couldn't make it. I can't think of a thing to say. I have no idea how people do this. I think I might be the most boring human alive.

'Cheers, hen,' says the driver.

'Thanks – bye,' I say. And as I step off the bus I realize that – a head taller than anyone else surrounding him – I can see Ed walking down the pavement towards me with his loping walk, which looks casual, but covers the ground incredibly fast. He's got a dark brown Labrador trotting beside him.

He raises a hand in greeting, and I feel my stomach dropping through the floor.

We are only walking a dog, I tell myself, and I lift my hand in a shy sort of wave.

He raises his hand again, and I realize he's grinning, and somehow it makes me feel better. I hitch my bag over my shoulder.

I've shoved some lunch things in my rucksack – I wasn't sure what to bring, but when I stopped at the shop this morning I picked up a pack of Oreos, because they made me smile.

'Hey.' He smiles.

'Hi.'

We both stand there for a moment. I bend down to stroke his dog.

'Meg,' he says, 'meet Holly.'

Meg sits down obediently on hearing her name. She looks up at me, her dark brown eyes gentle, and I rub behind her ears. She lifts a paw and I shake it.

'Hello, Meg.'

'She's very well brought up, as you can see.'

'Of course she is.' I look up at Ed, who is smiling broadly.

'Naturally.'

'So,' I straighten up. 'What d'you want to do?'

Ed rubs his chin. 'Country park?'

There's a path through the woods that leads up to the back of the country park. It's owned by the Laird of

Hopetoun, but the land is for everyone to use.

'OK.' I feel another flutter of nerves in my stomach.

'Can you just hold this for a sec?' He passes me Meg's red leather lead, shrugs off the green plaid shirt he's wearing, and ties it round his waist.

It's hot, and I'm in a black cardigan and a purple vest, but I've just remembered I forgot to put on sun cream. If I take it off, I'll be burned in about half an hour. I'll just have to bake.

'Ready?' He holds out his hand.

I pass Meg's lead back to him, and we set off, side by side. He can't seem to think of anything to say either. It's silence, but not a companionable one. It feels more like we've forgotten how to have a conversation, and I can't believe we are the same two people who sat by the canal chatting and laughing just the other day.

We walk up the high street, past the little coffee and book shop I love to browse in on the way home from swimming. Inside, the American tourist group has taken over three tables, and they're all looking at a map and drinking Cokes.

'Do you want a lolly?' Ed says, surprising me. He sticks a hand in his pocket and pulls out a fiver, brandishing it in the air. 'I'm boiling, aren't you?'

'Melting.'

I pretend to mop my brow and realize I look like a complete idiot. He heads inside, and Meg looks up at me.

'I have no idea,' I say to her.

She pants, not very helpfully.

'I got one orange and one lemonade,' says Ed. 'I realize I should have asked which one you wanted. Sorry. You do like one of those, don't you?'

And I realize that actually maybe he's as nervous as me.

'I like both.'

'Which one d'you want?'

'You choose.'

He shakes his head and laughs, and I notice again how straight his teeth are, and how white.

'You.'

'Orange, then, please.'

The path up to the country park is narrow and lined with stinging nettles, which don't seem to bother Meg. Once we've clambered over the stile, and Meg's ducked under the little dog-access slot, Ed lets her off the lead, and she lumbers on ahead of us, her head down and tail up. She's so much slower and more considered than Rio's dog Blue, who hurtles everywhere at top speed. Meg seems totally laid back. Thinking of Rio and Ed, I realize that there must be something in the dogs-being-like-their-owners thing.

'What are you smiling at?' Ed looks sideways at me.

We've been walking along eating our lollies, but they're done now.

'Just thinking about dogs and their owners.'

'You think I'm like Meg?'

'You're both smiley,' I say.

Ed gives a nod and looks pleased. 'She's a nice dog to be compared to, I reckon.'

'How old is she?'

'Two.'

'That's . . .' I try to remember how old that makes her in dog years.

'Eight,' Ed says, apparently reading my mind. 'I got her when she was ten weeks old. She was a present from my mum.'

'I've always wanted a dog, but our house is too small.'

'Ours is now, really.' He takes the lollipop stick from my hand and throws it in a bin as we pass one. 'But I used to –'

He stops, and a look I can't recognize flashes across his face.

'Used to what?'

'Oh, just – we used to have a bigger house. Before we moved.'

'From Edinburgh?'

We fork left, following the signpost that says 'Stone Cairn', and head up the hill into the forest.

'Yep.'

I get the feeling he doesn't want to talk about it. There's a weird sort of silence that falls as we make our way up the steepest part of the path. The rocks are loose, and the track pitted by the mountain bikers who hurtle down the hill in all weathers. The thin soles of my sneakers aren't exactly protective, and I can feel the rough edges of the flints against my feet.

'Ow!' I gasp, feeling the ground shifting slightly underneath me. I lose my footing and grab on to Ed's arm without thinking.

'Steady,' he says.

He has swimmer's arms – muscular and strong – and I pull myself upright.

'Shall we stop for a bit?'

I let go of his arm, turning to look down the way we've just walked. My ankle twinges a bit, and for a second I have visions of returning home to Mum with mine in a matching cast, but I think I just twisted it slightly. I sit down on the grass edge of the path. Meg trots back to check on me, sniffing my leg before sitting down beside me. I put an arm round her neck. We're both out of breath.

'I don't remember this path being so steep,' Ed says with a look of concern.

I rub my ankle for a moment. 'It's just this bit. It levels out in a second.'

'Are you OK to keep going? Is your ankle OK?'

I give my foot an experimental wiggle. Meg hefts herself upright as well, and echoes me by giving herself a shake.

'I think she likes you.'

'I like her too. And it's fine. Once we get over the top bit there –' I motion to a group of pine trees where the path appears to stop – 'there's a little picnic area.'

'Shame we don't have any Oreos.' Ed catches my eye for a second.

'Funnily enough . . .' I pat the shoulder strap of my rucksack.

He laughs.

We're sitting on the picnic bench, halfway up the hill to the stone cairn that was put there years ago by the Laird of Something to celebrate his success in the Battle of

Something Else. If I'd paid more attention to the teachers every time we'd been dragged up here on a school trip, I'd know a lot more about it.

'So.' Ed looks at me.

I feel the strangest sensation in my knees. And my stomach. In fact, I feel quite strange all over. I am alone, with a boy (and a dog, but she's digging a hole under an oak tree), and there's nobody here but us.

I watch him as he leans forward, putting his chin in his hand, and looking at me intently.

'Tell me something about you.'

It sounds like a cheesy line from a movie. I raise a sceptical eyebrow, and he lifts his in acknowledgement. Yes, it's a line. But I guess, at the end of the day, everything's a cliché, really.

'Like what?'

I notice that his eyes aren't quite brown or green. They're a mixture of both, ringed with dark grey. And then I look down, because I realize I've been looking at his eyes and not saying anything and I feel weirdly nervous.

'Tell me something nobody else knows.'

He's surprisingly intense. His gaze doesn't waver, and he looks at me steadily.

'Nobody else in the whole world?'

It feels like time has stopped and there's just us. There's no sound anywhere but the whispering of the wind in the trees.

'Nobody else.'

I think for a moment. And there's a second when I think

about the house, and Mum, and all the stuff at home. And I think about the fact that I don't tell anyone any of that stuff. But now isn't the time. I don't want it to be about all of that.

'OK,' I say, and I look at him and echo his pose, leaning forward, my chin cupped in both hands. 'One thing.'

Ed leans forward. 'Go on.' His eyebrows raise a fraction.

'You promise you won't tell a soul?' I lower my voice.

'Not a living soul.' His eyes are dark.

I lean forward a bit closer. I feel not quite like myself. It's the strangest, most dizzying feeling. I feel like . . . like someone is actually listening to me. And like it wouldn't really matter what I said.

I lower my voice. 'You know *Lord of the Flies*?'

He nods – well, he sort of nods with his eyebrows, his chin still in his hands, his eyes still on me.

'I haven't read it at all.'

And Ed gives a shout of laughter.

Emboldened, I carry on. 'And I haven't a clue what Castle Rock is.'

'Oh God,' he says, and he sits up, arching his back and stretching his arms upward, linking his hands together behind his head. He grins at me. 'You were so bloody serious there. I thought you were going to tell me you were a secret serial killer.'

'Oh, I'm that as well,' I say, laughing. 'I've lured you up here to your doom.'

I have no idea who this new version of me is. I like her, though.

'Your turn.'

'Hmmm,' says Ed as Meg reappears, a strand of sticky willow hanging round her throat like a necklace. He pulls it from her and drops it on the ground at her feet.

'Go on,' I say. 'And then you can tell me what Castle Rock is and if I should read *Lord of the Flies* and what your favourite book is.'

'Deal.' Ed casts his eyes upward as he thinks. 'OK . . . Something about me nobody else knows . . .'

But before he can carry on, there's a crash as Meg leaps forward, her hackles raised, and she growls and snarls at a man who emerges from the gloom on the other side of the clearing. He's in a pair of running shorts and a bright yellow vest. Ed stiffens as well, and for a second he doesn't move, watching the man as he draws closer.

'Meg,' he says, clicking his fingers, and motioning her back to his side. 'It's fine.'

'All right?' says the runner.

He has close cropped dark hair and a triangle of sweat on the back of his vest, and we all three watch as he makes his way down the path we've just climbed up, fleet-footed, nimble and fast.

'What was that about?'

Ed leans down and pats Meg. 'Nothing,' he says, and looks back at me. But I don't feel convinced. I've spend too much of my life covering up not to recognize it in other people.

'Shall we head up to the cairn?' I say.

Ed swings his legs round from the picnic bench.

The cairn is surrounded by people who've approached it from the other side – the visitors' side. People balance on the edge of the stones with selfie sticks, taking photographs, and up here all the picnic tables are taken. The food I've brought stays in my bag. Meg tries to investigate the contents of someone's picnic basket, and Ed has to pull her away, apologizing.

'I'm awfully sorry,' he says, and the family, charmed by his lovely manners, shake their heads and tell him it's fine, not a problem.

'You're so posh,' I say as we start walking down the path away from the crowds.

'I'm really not.'

'Oh come on.' I look at him sceptically. 'I've never met anyone who says "I'm awfully sorry" before.'

'I've never met anyone who hasn't read *Lord of the Flies* before.' He grins at me and nudges me with his elbow.

I shove him back. 'I've never met anyone who *has*. And I've never met anyone who has a dog called Meg.'

'I've never met anyone called Cressida.'

'All right,' I admit. 'Now Cressi is posh.'

'We can agree on that,' says Ed, and he blows his floppy hair out of his eyes. It lifts up for a second, then lands back exactly where it was.

'I am so hot,' he says, and collapses down on the grassy bank by the path. He lies back, sitting up on his elbows, and looks up at me. 'Aren't you melting in that jumper?'

'Cardigan.'

'Whatever.' He laughs. 'It's the hottest day Scotland has ever experienced, we're melting thanks to global warming and you're in a woolly jump– sorry, *cardigan*.'

I pull one shoulder free, showing the strap of my vest top. My pale skin is covered in freckles. 'If I take it off, I'll burn in about five minutes.'

'Why don't we walk down that way, then?' Ed points down the hill, where there's a little path that leads through the shade of the trees. 'If you die of heatstroke, I'm going to have some explaining to do. Your parents will have to come and collect you, and I'll be in for it.'

In for it. I smile to myself.

'Parent.' I say. 'Singular.'

'Oh,' he says, scrambling back up. He brushes pine needles and grass off his knees, looking up at me all the while.

'There's just me and my mum.' I've explained this so many times. People still find the idea that there's no father in our equation almost impossible to understand.

'Are your parents divorced?'

I shake my head. 'Shall we go?' I say, pointing towards the woods.

We head into the shade provided by the tree canopy, and the pine-smelling darkness is a relief. I'm not designed for baking-hot sunshine. I rub my forehead, realizing it's damp with sweat. My hair is sticking to the back of my neck, and I lift it up in a handful, waving it up and down so a tiny breeze blows down the back of my T-shirt.

'There's just the two of us.' I realize he's still waiting

for me to reply. 'I don't know my dad.'

We walk on a bit. I shrug off my cardigan and ball it up in my hand.

'There's just me and my mum too.' He chews on the inside of his lip before he continues. 'Well, and Meg. She counts, don't you, Meggie?'

Hearing his voice, Meg spins round, tail wagging hopefully.

I smile. 'She definitely counts.'

'No brothers or sisters?'

I think of Lauren, and of the box room at home, all ready for her to stay in later this week. 'It's – complicated.'

Ed looks at me with a puzzled expression, his brows knitting together. He opens his mouth to speak, then closes it again, then raises a hand palm up in a gesture of confusion. 'Complicated?'

I screw up my face. 'There used to be four of us. I have an ex-stepsister.'

Ed nods slowly. 'Right.'

I echo his nod. 'That's what I mean by complicated.'

He smiles his big smile at me. 'Families are really weird.'

We turn, together, and start walking again.

'Oh yes,' I say.

With my cardigan off, the sensation that I've had a layer of protection removed is even more intense. I feel like every crackle of twigs breaking underfoot and the muffled sounds of Meg galloping ahead of us have been turned up to full volume. We're walking close enough that I'm aware the whole time of his physical presence, and of mine. I've never been so aware of my body. And I wonder as we're walking if he feels the same way. Or is he thinking we're out for a perfectly nice walk as friends, and I'm imagining all of this? What if we never actually – I mean, I don't know how anyone ever actually –

His arm brushes against mine as the path narrows, and his skin against mine feels like it crackles with static.

'Sorry,' I say, even though all we did was touch slightly.

He says it too.

And then we walk on a bit in a silence that feels heavy and thick. My mind is racing. I imagine what it would be like to just turn round right there in the woods and the silence and kiss him.

There's no sound, but my heart is thudding so hard because I keep thinking about what it would be like to be the sort of person to just kiss someone and wondering how people like that learn to do that sort of thing, or does it just sort of happen, or –

'Hello again,' says the jogging man from earlier, panting into view from behind a bush.

We both jump, and I stand there for a second as he runs off, my hand on my heart. Ed is doubled over laughing. It's broken the weird silence.

'Penny for your thoughts?'

It's such an old-fashioned thing to say.

'Mine are much more expensive than that,' I say, thinking as I do that there's no way I'm going to tell him what I was actually thinking.

'I've got –' he reaches into his pocket and pulls out a

handful of coins – 'two pounds and forty-three pence.'

'I'm so sorry,' I say, teasing. 'I'm afraid my thoughts start at two fifty and go up from there.'

'Half a thought?'

'Nope.'

'Mine are a lot cheaper.'

I raise my eyebrows and laugh. 'Really?'

'Oh God, yes – I'm easy. A chocolate biscuit, and I'm all yours.'

I stop and pull my rucksack off my shoulder. 'Funny you should mention that.'

There's a fallen log by the side of the path, and I sit down on it for a moment. Ed stands in front of me, looking down. I notice the hole in the toe of his shoe again.

'I just happen to have –' I pull the packet of Oreos and two cans of Coke out of my bag – 'several chocolate – well, chocolate-ish – biscuits right here.'

Ed sits down on the opposite end of the maskeshift bench. I feel like I'm a million miles from my life, and yet home is just a few miles away. But the person I am here – is this the me I'd be all the time if things weren't so difficult? It's the strangest thought.

'So –' I tear open the top of the packet and hold a biscuit up in my hand – 'one biscuit, one thought?'

Ed holds his hand out, palm up. His eyes are twinkling and he looks like he's about to laugh.

'Uh-uh.' I shake my head, teasing. 'Thought first.' I pull it back towards my chest.

He rubs his chin thoughtfully. I feel a jolt of anticipation shoot through me, and the hairs on my bare arms stand up.

'I was thinking,' Ed begins, looking at me with a level gaze, 'that you're the first person I've met since I moved here that makes me laugh.'

I look directly into his green-brown eyes, and for a beat of silence neither of us says a word. It's as if the world is holding its breath.

I place a biscuit on his outstretched hand and wait. He takes it, twists it in half and gives me one section. As he passes it to me, our hands touch again and I catch his eye and I wonder if it's not my imagination after all. He looks away.

'Look at Meg.' She's trotting back up the path towards us. 'She can smell a biscuit from about five miles away.'

'Can she have one?' I'm still holding my half in my hand, because my stomach is turning over and over with a weird mixture of nerves and excitement.

'One. Dogs aren't meant to have chocolate. I don't know if an Oreo counts.'

I give her my half, and she wolfs it down in a gulp.

'She's supposed to be on a strict diet, but she keeps escaping through the fence into next door's garden. The other day she came back with half a packet of sausages hanging out of her mouth.'

'Like a cartoon dog.'

We both laugh.

'Exactly.'

Meg mooches around the floor and looks for crumbs,

but there aren't any. She wanders off, bored.

'Can I have another one?' Ed leans forward, his elbow resting on his knee, chin cupped in his hand, and looks at me.

'Thought?' I say, even though I know what he means.

'Biscuit.' He gives me a smile that says, *You know what I mean.*

'Go on, then.' I take it out and hold it in mid-air, like a disc.

'I was wondering why you come here to swim when there's a perfectly good pool in Kilmuir.'

I keep hold of the Oreo.

'Because you're here, obviously,' I tease.

'Very good.' He looks a bit pleased, even though he knows I'm joking. I think he might even be blushing, and that makes me feel – bolder. Braver.

'Seriously, though . . .' Ed leans in slightly closer towards me, as if inviting a confidence.

'I don't exactly . . .' I look for another way of saying it that sounds less like the other me, and more like this interesting, new version of myself, but I can't find one.

'Fit?' Ed says gently.

'Yes,' I say.

I shift my position on the log, feeling exposed and awkward. It's not something that I've said aloud before – somehow joking about being the socially awkward outcasts with Rio and Allie feels different to admitting it out loud.

'Well,' he says, and he reaches forward to gently take the packet from my hands, 'I guess that's something else we have in common.'

I watch my fingers loosen their grip and his hand next to mine. He's moved closer to reach them, and he doesn't move back. He has freckles on his nose that I hadn't noticed before, and his dark hair is damp with sweat and curling over one eye. I feel like my heart is beating so hard in my chest that at any moment it might burst out.

Then there's a soft thud as something falls from the trees and lands on the log between us. As one, we both jump up to standing. My heart is pounding, and Ed's so close that I can feel the heat of his skin through his T-shirt, and there's a split second where – because we're both as tall as the other – our eyes meet and it could go one way . . . We could step back and pretend that this hadn't happened . . . or –

I don't move. And neither does he. I can sense his chest rising and falling. I can see the smattering of freckles on his nose and the black of his eyebrows and my nose is almost touching his. I lean into him and somehow he inclines his head at exactly the same moment and his mouth is on mine. My hands are by my sides and I feel them balling into fists for a second and then I reach up and curl my arm round his waist as he lifts a hand to my hair and –

Ed pauses for a second and I feel his lips curling against mine in a smile.

'Sorry.' He pulls away slightly.

'No,' I say, and I pull him back towards me.

Meg interrupts us, eventually, weaving between our legs and knocking us sideways so I topple slightly and Ed's hand on my hip is the only thing that stops me falling back against the log.

'It's a bird's nest,' he says, looking over my shoulder.

I turn around. On the ground there's a faded grey woven jumble of twigs and leaves.

'We should keep it as a memento.' Ed grins.

'A bird might need it.'

'I think they might be a bit late, somehow. It's June.'

He swings my hand in his and I feel shy for a second. I bite my lip.

'So –' I begin.

'Here we are,' says Ed, but he looks me directly in the eye and raises his chin slightly, as if challenging me.

'Penny for your thoughts, you said.'

I look at the empty Oreo packet lying on the ground, and we realize at the same moment that Meg has wolfed down the rest of them when we weren't looking.

'I was thinking –' he reaches over to tuck an unruly curl behind my ear, and the coolness of his fingers rests for a second on my neck before he runs his hand down my arm to lace his fingers between mine – 'that I wanted to kiss you.'

And he leans into me again, his mouth brushing against mine for just a second before he takes a step back, holding both my hands and lifting them up so we look as if we're about to dance, or wrestle, as if he's sizing me up.

'But I kissed you instead.'

'I don't think so,' he says, laughing and pulling me close for a moment. 'I was definitely the kisser.'

'You were not,' I say into the side of his hair. His dark curls smell of something lemony and fresh.

'Was too.'

He pulls back and goes to kiss me on the mouth, but I duck my head at the wrong moment and he misses, the kiss landing on the tip of my nose, which makes us both laugh.

'Let's go before we get attacked by any more flying birds nests,' I say. I feel like I need to take a breath to digest what's just happened.

We start walking back down the hill through the trees. For five minutes or so, we walk along in silence – but a good sort of silence. It feels like the kind when you stop holding your breath. Ed's holding my hand, and Meg – tired now – is ambling just ahead of us. It feels right.

I hitch the strap of my vest top back up on my bare shoulder and realize with a start –

'My bag.' It's got everything in it – my keys, my phone. 'Where is it?'

'I think it's by the fallen log.' I turn to head back up the hill.

'You wait there; I'll run back up.'

'Are you sure?'

He grins at me. 'Course.'

I watch as he runs up the hill, following the path as it curves and then dips so he disappears out of sight. Meg wavers for a second, looking at me and then at him, then canters off. I'm alone for a moment and I spin round, hearing the crack of a branch echoing through the silence.

There's nobody there.

I stand on tiptoe, trying to see where they've gone. And for a second I feel my stomach drop and the feeling sneaks in again. I remember being last to be chosen for the team in PE last week and the look on Lauren's face as she stood watching me as the team captains picked – one by one by one – everyone in our set until I was the only one left.

And for a fleeting moment, I think maybe Ed's realized that he's made a terrible mistake and I'm standing here alone, again.

And then his dark head comes into view, his arm aloft, holding the bag. And Meg comes hurtling down the path towards me and I bend down to welcome her with open arms and I realize that sometimes good things can happen . . . even to me.

CHAPTER TWELVE

When I get ready for school on Monday morning, I look at my reflection and trace a finger round the outline of my mouth and remember that it wasn't just my imagination. It was real.

I decide not to tell Allie and Rio, even though they've saved a space for me at lunch and are asking what I've been up to. I half expected everyone to know already – for the head teacher to pull me up in assembly and say, 'Right, everyone, we've got an announcement to make – Holly Gilmour has kissed a boy, and not just once, either.'

'So what did you do in Edinburgh?' I ask them.

'My dad sold four paintings, so he gave us thirty quid to go and do whatever we wanted.'

'And we went up to the Meadows and bought pizza and pretended to be students and someone asked us directions.' Allie preens slightly. She's completely obsessed with the idea of being a student in Edinburgh. 'They were going for an open day and they thought we were at the university.' She flashes a grin of genuine delight.

'And I got a ton of stuff in the sale,' says Rio.

'Hence the smell,' says Allie, shoving him with her elbow so he sways forward and I catch a throat-tightening

126

whiff of about five different artificial man-smells. It makes me think of Ed's hair and the faintest scent of lime and my stomach tightens in excitement and nerves. 'What did you do?'

'Me?' I look down at the floor, swinging one leg and tracing circles on the wood with my toe. 'Nothing, really. Worked. Went for a walk.'

'You could've come with us.'

'I was getting the box room ready for a house guest.' I realize they don't know the whole story.

I lean in and explain, quietly, that Lauren – currently sitting on the opposite side of the room with Madison and the rest of the gang – is coming to stay, and why.

'Bloody hell!' Allie's jaw drops open and her eyes pop wide.

She does a comedy double take from Madison's table back to me.

'You –' she raises her eyebrows – 'are going to be having her as a house guest?'

She turns to Rio, her audience. For a split second I wonder if he's going to join in and start booing. I realize that to them Lauren's one of those people – the ones who've studiously avoided making friends with them. The ones who make them feel uncomfortable because they don't conform to the same identikit pattern as everyone else.

'Yes.'

'And how do you feel about it?'

I poke at the plastic lid of my coffee cup. 'Lauren's

OK when she's not with them.'

Allie's eyebrows shoot up skywards.

Rio chokes on a mouthful of coffee. 'Seriously?'

Allie looks unimpressed. 'What was it she called us?'

'*Social rejects*,' says Rio, doing a passable impression of Lauren's high-pitched voice, flicking his imaginary hair over his shoulder.

'Lauren said that?' I can't quite believe it.

'Not her – the other one.' Allie flicks a glance in their direction. 'Madison. Queen Bee.'

'Lauren's not really like that. Honestly.'

I feel awkward. I'm defending her, but I can feel the atmosphere is uncomfortable and weird.

'God. Sorry,' says Allie. 'I'm being tactless again. I'm sure she can't be completely awful if she's related to you – or close enough.'

The thing is, Allie doesn't have any idea about Lauren and Neil being part of our family. She was still living in Birmingham when they moved out and into Clare's huge house down on the shore. And it must be pretty weird to think of someone like Lauren being sisters with me.

'She's not all that bad,' I surprise myself by saying.

We're not allowed to check our phones in school. If we're caught with them out, they're confiscated and can't be returned unless a parent comes to the office to sign them out. Mine is in my bag, on silent, and I am aching to check it.

'Miss,' I say, midway through RE. 'Can I just . . . ?' I look at my bag fleetingly, and then widen my eyes imploringly.

'Do you need to be excused?' says Miss Thomson.

She's the one teacher I know will fall for the 'I've got my period' excuse without fail. She's lovely, but this is her first year teaching, and she still hasn't worked out that most of the girls in her class must have major gynaecological issues if they all have their period when they say they do.

I pick up my bag and slide out of my chair. Normally I wouldn't draw attention to myself like this, but I need to check my phone. I go to the bathroom, lock the cubicle door and switch it on.

It's not silent and it bleeps so loudly when it comes to life that I expect a flock of teachers to appear, peering over the top of the door.

Ed: 3 New Messages, the screen says. I sit down on the lid of the loo. The mobile reception in here is awful and I can't connect to the school Wi-Fi, but after a second it connects to the Messenger app.

Morning.

He'd sent that in reply to mine, which was typed from Cressi's car.

I would have written more than *Hi, hope you have a nice day* if she hadn't peered over my shoulder at a junction and asked to whom it was, and if I had 'a significant other' with a knowing look. I'd said no, and felt my cheeks stinging red, switched my phone off and stared out of the window for the rest of the journey, listening to the host of the Radio 2 breakfast show chattering away and the swish of the windscreen wipers in the rain.

***What are you doing later? Are you coming up
to the pool tonight? x***

And the third message, sent at break:

***This is the longest day ever. Wish it was
yesterday x***

I feel the corners of my mouth turning up in a smile,
which stays on my face as I type my reply.

Me too. I'm teaching 4 to 6, and then I'm free.

And then just before I hit send, I type

x

And it makes me smile even more. Because, later
tonight, I can kiss him for real.

I'm still smiling when I walk back into the classroom and
take my seat.

I stop smiling a second later when Miss Thomson's
lecture on women's rights in Northern Ireland comes to
an end at exactly the same time as my phone – which
I'd forgotten to turn off in my excitement – bleeps and
vibrates in my bag on the floor.

The class is silent.

'Whose phone was that?' Miss Thomson casts her eyes
about the room.

There's a shuffling of feet, and several people cast
surreptitious glances at their bags.

'Quiet.' She sounds surprisingly fierce, and we all sit
there for a second.

'You gonna search all our bags, miss?'

She shakes her head, thin-lipped. 'Hardly, Michael.'

I sit for the remaining twenty minutes of the lesson with my fingers crossed, begging my phone not to give me away.

'You home straight after swimming?' Mum calls to me in the hall as I pick up my bus pass.

'Might be a bit late. Depends if Cressi needs me to cover an extra class. In fact –' I cover my back – 'I might stay and have a swim.'

'Text me and let me know when you're on the way,' she says.

'You're looking very smart this evening,' says Cressi, looking up from her clipboard.

I tug at the collar of my council-issued polo shirt. We've all been given new ones. Navy blue for the qualified teachers, and orange for the assistants. Orange, which clashes so badly with my hair that just looking in the mirror makes me want to hide forever.

'Smart?'

'Put it this way: we're not going to lose you.'

'Cheers for that.' I shake my head. Maybe it'll look less awful when I get in the water.

'Holly!' says Theo, one of the terror twins, waving.

It's not their day for a lesson. At least there's that. I raise a hand briefly and wave.

'We're here for swimming lessons again,' says Ezra, the other half of the duo.

They're identical in green swimming trunks and bright

blue goggles. If it wasn't for their named swimming caps, I wouldn't have a clue who I was talking to.

'Mummy's changed the day.'

'And you're here!' chirps Theo, shoving his brother so he slips on the tiled floor. 'Hooray.'

I grit my teeth in a smile. 'Hooray.'

'Boys, you go and sit down over there.' Cressi points at the bench by the edge of the pool. Her sergeant-major tones are far more effective than my attempts – they actually listen to her and sit relatively politely, waiting for the rest of the group.

The time passes quickly. It's funny how a day at school can drag so much, but hours in the pool can go by in moments. Despite the twins (who refused to listen to me, and ended up 'helping' Cressi by the side of the pool for the second half of the lesson), I enjoy teaching the little ones. There's something really nice about knowing that you're sharing something you love.

'You all right?'

I hear the voice and turn round reflexively, realizing before I see his face that it's Ed. He's standing in front of me, his hair hanging in dark, wet waves over his eyes. He pushes it back and smiles at me. His long eyelashes are starfish spikes.

I put a hand to my hair, forgetting that it's tied back. And I can't help it. I smile back at him and the orangeness of my shirt is forgotten.

'Edward –' Cressi raises a hand – 'you angling for a job?'

'Perhaps,' he says, and his cheeks dimple as he smiles

at her and ducks his head, looking adorably shy for a second. He turns back to me. 'What time did you say you finish?'

I don't know what to do with myself. I tug at the hem of my awful orange polo shirt and try to ignore the fact that he's once again standing in front of me – topless – only now I've kissed him and I feel like my face is tomato coloured with embarrassment and everyone in the entire pool is looking at me. I look up at the big clock at the end of the pool.

'Half an hour.'

'I thought I'd swim until you were done. Cool. See you outside?'

I nod, biting my lip.

Cressi looks across at me, her eyebrows raised. 'You done?'

'Coming.'

Ed dives into the pool, disappearing out of sight and re-emerging halfway down. I head back over to the side of the pool, picking up the clipboard to check the numbers of the next class.

'He must have been in a team, your Edward.'

The blush that was dissipating flares up again, and I can feel my cheeks are burning hot. 'He's not *my* Edward.'

Cressi's nostrils flare and her eyebrows rise at the same time. She gives a snort of disbelief. 'He looks like it from where I'm standing.'

'We're just friends.'

'Course you are.' She barks a laugh like a sea lion and

turns back to the children who are lined up neatly by the side of the pool. 'Right, then. Backstroke.'

Afterwards – having tamed my hair with half a bottle of conditioner in the shower and smudged some eyeliner and mascara on – I roll my swimming stuff up in my bag and head out into the foyer of the pool. Ed's sitting, his long legs splayed out, reading a book. He's far too big for the chair in the waiting area. When he sees me standing with my hand on the door of the changing rooms, he springs up, shoving the book in his back pocket, and runs a hand through his shaggy still-damp hair.

'You're the only person I know who actually carries a book around,' I say, and I can feel my whole self smiling. It's such a strange feeling.

He's in a pair of faded jeans and a different plaid shirt, and a washed-out grey T-shirt with a fox logo on the front. He wears clothes as if they're an afterthought. As if he doesn't care that they're all a bit small on him. But the strange thing is that I recognize the fox logo as being one of the expensive designers Rio loves, and the plaid shirt is Abercrombie. His too-small clothes aren't like my Primark ones: they're like him – sort of posh, but casual about it, somehow.

'What d'you want to do?' he says.

'I don't mind.' I feel like my entire brain has been overtaken by the urge to just kiss him right there in the middle of the foyer. As if all the parts of me that normally think sensible thoughts, the ones that have spent the last few years trying to hold things together, are completely rebelling. I take his hand, and he gives me a smile of surprise.

'Hello.' He swings my hand in his.

'Hi.' I smile back. 'Do you want to go for a walk?' It comes out sounding so unlikely that I pull a face.

He looks at me and raises his eyebrows for a second, and he looks so like a disapproving teacher that I burst out laughing.

'I mean an *actual* walk.'

'Oh.' His face falls. 'I liked the one we did yesterday.'

I feel myself fizzing all over again. 'Me too.'

He stops walking for a second before me, and the momentum spins me round so I'm facing him. He takes a step forward and puts his hand in the small of my back and before I know what's happening I'm kissing him, on the pavement, in the middle of the car park.

I pull back, laughing.

'A walk,' I say, in admonishment.

'Absolutely.' His turned-down trying-not-to-laugh smile is incredibly cute.

'Come on, then,' I say, and tugging his hand I march ahead.

'It's not often I meet someone who can keep up with me,' Ed says as we walk along the road to the shop.

'I've got long legs,' I say, lifting one foot up and wiggling it in the air.

'You do.'

'Where d'you want to go?'

I look along the high street. The rain has stopped at last, and the evening sun has come out, polishing the tops of the buildings with gold. I catch a glimpse of the castle beyond the facades of the shops that line the street.

'Do you want to walk round the loch?'

'Is it open at this time of night?' Ed cocks his head to one side.

'No,' I say, with a mischievous raise of one eyebrow. 'But I have ways.'

'Go on, then,' he says, and he swings my hand again. 'This sounds interesting.'

We walk past the chip shop and my stomach growls. I think – if ever it was needed – this must be proof that I'll never be the sort of person who loses their appetite. Swimming always leaves me ravenous, even when I'm walking hand in hand with a boy.

'Shall we get some?' I dig into the pocket of my jeans and pull out the fiver I stuffed there earlier.

'I thought you'd never ask.' Ed smiles.

As we wait for the next batch to cook, we lean against the green-and-white-tiled wall.

'Oh God,' says Ed, pointing at one of the notices pinned to the wall.

There's a photograph of a wedding dress glued to the corner of a handwritten index card: '*For sale. Never worn.*'

'Maybe she decided on a different style.' I lean forward and peer at the picture. 'It looks a bit old-fashioned.'

'Maybe she . . . disappeared.' Ed waggles his eyebrows.

'Maybe she changed her mind at the last minute and

went travelling round the world, and left him with the dress as a memento.'

'I read a thing about that once,' Ed says, and he looks thoughtful for a moment. 'It was in the paper, I think.'

'Look at this one.' I point to another scrap of paper. *'Half-finished bottle of Bell's Whisky – £7?'*

'Maybe they're having a clear-out.'

I read out another. *'Four lawnmowers, all perfect condition.'*

'Authentic as real baby-doll and outfits . . .' It's Ed's turn to peer at the wall, and then he takes my elbow and pulls me in so I can inspect it too.

There's a photograph of what looks like a newborn baby, and a heap of pink and purple frilly dresses, and they're lying on top of what looks like the bonnet of an ancient brown Volvo.

'What the . . . ?' I pull a face.

'It takes all sorts, my granny used to say.'

I shake my head. We're both trying not to laugh now.

'Don't ask . . .'

'Two chips?'

The sullen-faced woman behind the counter has completely ignored our rising hysterics.

'Salt and sauce?'

'Yes please,' we say together.

'So, teach me the ways of the secret path,' Ed says, following me between the Spar and the little bookshop on the high street.

We've decided to keep our chips wrapped in their bags until we get to the loch, and I've promised him that I'll show him how we get into the locked National Trust land after hours.

'It shuts at five,' I explain. 'But you can climb over the wall down here where it collapsed a couple of years ago when there was a flood. They didn't bother fixing it . . . Hold these a second.' I scramble over the wooden gate, ignoring the sign that says 'No Entry – Private Land'.

'You're surprisingly rebellious,' Ed says, and I think he sounds approving.

'I have hidden depths.'

I reach over and take the hot paper parcels of chips from his hands, and he clambers over the gate after me. We make our way down the side of an empty field, which is overgrown with thistles and yellow ragwort, and I give a showman's bow as I present the fallen-down wall to him.

'So nobody knows about this?'

'I think they probably figure the only people who'll come down here at this time of night are locals.' I think of the American tourists I saw the other day, their necks strewn with binoculars and expensive cameras. They wouldn't risk climbing up here without a guidebook and a flask of hot coffee.

'So we have the entire loch to ourselves.' Ed spins around, taking in the view.

The thin evening sun is reflecting on the water, and the castle overlooks us from the hill – a stone skeleton that has stood guard over Hopetoun since the time when Mary

Queen of Scots was born here in 1542. There's an island in the middle, inhabited only by birds, and the path that meanders round the outside of the loch is almost three miles long, dotted with wooden exercise equipment and chairs dedicated to locals and visitors from all around the world who've loved spending time here. But this is the time I like it best. There's nobody here but us, and it's as if the place was built for us alone.

'I used to come here when I was little,' Ed says as we head for the nearest bench.

We sit down and open our chips, tearing at the damp paper.

'Me too.'

He grins. 'We might've been here at the same time.'

'Neil used to take me and Lauren at the weekends, sometimes, if Mum was teaching.'

'Lauren? She's your not-stepsister, right?'

'Yeah. And Neil's her dad – my not-stepdad. He's an idiot.'

Ed makes a noise of agreement through a mouthful of chips. 'Yeah, there's a lot of that about.'

I spin round on the bench so I'm facing him, tucking my legs up as if I was back in primary school, sitting tailor-fashion. I prop the chips on my ankles where they balance precariously.

'Idiots or stepdads?'

I don't know anything about Ed's family, except that he has a mum who doesn't take kindly to—

'Shit.'

'What is it?'

'I forgot to text my mum and let her know what I was doing. Hang on.' I pull my phone out of the pocket in my bag and send her a message.

Just hanging out for a bit. Will text when I'm on the bus. Won't be late.

The reply is instant.

Love you xxx

'Everything OK?'

'Yeah, she's pretty laid back in her own way. To be honest, she's been so wrapped up in her own stuff, she hasn't really been all that focused on –' I stop for a moment, realizing I'm making her sound like she's really shit at being a mum, and she's not. I pop a chip in my mouth and don't finish the sentence.

'My dad used to take me here too,' Ed says.

'Is he . . . ?'

I don't finish the sentence.

Ed shakes his head with a flat sort of smile. 'No – still very much here. I just don't have anything to do with him.'

I don't know quite what to say to that. Ed's chewing on the inside of his lip so his mouth twists sideways. His expression is thunderous.

'He's a dick.' He throws a chip across the path so it lands in the water. A duck flaps towards it and swallows it, whole.

'We moved here because of him. To get away from him.'

'I'm sorry,' I say.

'S'OK.' He shrugs and scuffs the ground with the toe of

his boot, making a sweeping arc in the gravel and exposing the dirt underneath. 'I'm less pissed off than I was before. But I still feel bad.'

'How d'you mean?'

'I feel like it's my fault. Like – I didn't know anything was going on until . . .'

He trails off. I don't quite know what to say. A silence falls and I can't work out if I should ask what he means. But if I do, and he starts asking me what's going on in my life, I don't even know where I'd begin. I nibble on the end of a chip and watch as a pair of swans sail past.

'So what about your sister-not-sister?'

Uh-oh.

'Lauren?'

'Yeah.'

I don't want to go there. I guess we're both in the same place. I skirt around the issue, cautiously.

'We're not exactly the same sort of person.'

He raises an eyebrow. 'What sort of person is she?'

'Oh,' I begin, not thinking. 'Expensive designer clothes, loads of money, that sort of –' And then I stop, looking at Ed's Abercrombie shirt. His jeans have a rip in the knee, but, somehow, where mine are worn his look more like they were meant to be that way. It's as if he's sprouted six inches overnight and his limbs are growing out of the ends of his clothes. I can sympathize, because that's pretty much what happened to me a year or so back. Mum was in her shopping phase then, though, and an entire new wardrobe arrived (purchased with the credit card Neil paid off, mind you) in a courier van one afternoon. I haven't grown since then, and the stuff she bought is the same stuff I'm wearing now.

'And what sort of person are you?' Ed looks at me intently.

I've never really thought about that before.

'I'm—'

'Funny.'

'You think so?' I can feel myself smiling at the compliment.

'And kind.'

'Are we back to the Oreos again?'

'No.' Ed scrumples up the wrapper of his chips. He's managed to eat them in record time. Mine are stuck together in an unappetizing-looking mass.

'I watched you today when I was swimming,' he carries on. 'You're really nice to all those little kids.'

'That's because I remember being one myself.'

He grins. 'That's what most teachers forget.'

'Totally.' I think about school and breathe a sigh of relief. We're almost at the holidays, and then we can stop.

I look out across the still water of the lake and think for a moment. If you'd asked me a month ago, I'd have been able to tell you who I thought I was. I was Holly, who was just sixteen. Youngest in the year at school with a February birthday. Tallest in the class; taller than most of the boys. Red hair, long nose, white skin covered in freckles. Brown eyes. The one who always handed in homework on time in case she got into trouble. The one who tried to cover up what was happening at home because her mum was falling apart and—

'I don't really know what sort of person I am,' I say. 'But I think it's time to find out.'

I turn and drop the bag of chips in the bin beside the bench and shuffle along the bench so our legs are touching.

'Hello,' says Ed.

'I'm Holly,' I say.

His eyes crinkle up as he smiles at me.

'Lovely to make your acquaintance, Holly,' he says in his posh Edinburgh voice.

I look at him and wonder how I could have ever thought of him as weird-looking. His eyes seem to shift colour in the light – tonight they're more brown than green, and his pupils are deep black.

'How do you do,' I say in a posh voice.

He laughs, and instead of shaking my hand as he did the first time, he leans forward and tangles his hand in my hair and pulls me into a kiss.

By the time we've meandered around the loch, our shadows stretch out long in front of us. We've talked and kissed and talked, and I feel like I could stay up all night asking him questions about everything and never run out of things to say. But it's half nine, and the last bus is at ten to.

We stand at the bus stop with two old ladies who have armfuls of M&S bags.

'Let me help you with those,' says Ed as the bus groans to a stop in front of us. He takes the bags from the women and hops on to the bus, putting them down in the luggage rack before hopping back off again.

'I'll see you,' he says, and I lift my face to his for one last kiss. I don't want the evening to end.

I watch from the window of the bus as he stands waving, still smiling his big smile, his eyebrows framing his face. I want to jump back off the bus and stay in this world, the world over the hill where I am completely myself.

'You've got a keeper there, hen,' says one of the old women to me as I stand up.

'Aye.' The other one nods. 'Lovely manners. A proper gentleman.'

They both cackle with laughter as I feel my face going scarlet. I duck my head in acknowledgement and sway down the aisle to the front door of the bus.

CHAPTER THIRTEEN

It's a week into the holidays, and Neil's here, dropping off Lauren. 'You're looking well,' he says, grinning widely at me.

I swear he can tell there's something different about me. He gave me a funny look as soon as he got out of the car. And Mum said this morning she thought I looked happy. I don't know whether to be glad that having some sort of life means I look cheerful, or concerned that it means my normal face looks like the end of the world is nigh.

Lauren's standing in the hall with a chic-looking travel suitcase at her feet and what looks like some sort of make-up holdall over her shoulder. She *would* have a special case for carrying all her MAC stuff. My make-up comes from Superdrug and is shoved in an old toilet bag with the pattern all faded on the side where the sun shines on it on the bathroom window ledge.

'I really appreciate this, Fi,' Neil is saying. He peels off a wodge of twenty-pound notes, which he's taken out of his back pocket. 'Just to keep you lot going. I don't want you going without.'

'You don't have to,' Mum says haltingly.

I give her a fierce look. We've got no food in, and she

doesn't get her child benefit until tomorrow, and I for one am more than happy to spend Neil's money on a trip to Tesco to buy something for dinner that isn't freezer remnants. We've been living on that for the last five days after a bill came in that Mum had forgotten about. But there's a difference – she's been working out her finances with Cressi, sitting at the kitchen table with a spreadsheet on the ancient laptop that whirrs and groans and takes five minutes to come to life. It feels like maybe we might just make it. Especially if Neil's given us—

'Three hundred quid,' he says, handing over a wodge of notes to Mum. 'And here's a bit for you too, Holls. I've given Lauren some already. Don't want you two pulling hair and fighting like the old days.' He gives Mum a wink.

She shakes her head and catches my eye for a second afterwards, giving me a look that says, *Just humour him; he'll be gone soon.*

'Thanks,' I say, surprised. He's given me three brand-new twenty-pound notes. 'That's –' I stop for a second, looking sideways at Lauren, wondering how this makes her feel. I smile at Neil, and it's a genuine one tinged with relief that he's going, even if it does mean he's leaving Lauren here with us, and I have no idea how that's going to go. 'Thank you.'

'Holly's sorted the room out for you,' Mum says as Neil drops a kiss on Lauren's forehead and disappears – the door closing and silence falling instantly.

Her father brings a cloud of noise and performance with him wherever he goes – it's all an act, though. He's

146

all about show and having the right clothes and the right car and the right everything. It's no wonder that as soon as he got on his feet after he met Mum he started scouting around for someone to give him a foothold on the way up. He's always looking for more, more, most. I think that's why Lauren's always dressed the way she is. She's an accessory, like the posh car and the glamorous holiday to Barbados.

'Do you want to come up?' I feel shy all of a sudden. This was her home, and then it wasn't – and now it feels like she's on my territory, and she doesn't know how to handle it, and I'm not the sort of alpha person who knows how to claim it.

'OK.' She nods.

She's so quiet. I half expect her to unpack all her cronies from the travel bag and for the house to feel like the school common room does. I feel my stomach contract with nerves. For a second, I picture Madison in here, sitting on top of the faded duvet cover on the box-room bed, looking out at me with their blank stares and perfect hair and make-up. Thank God I can escape and spend time with Ed.

'You've still got Blue Teddy.' Lauren smiles at me, picking him up off the shelf.

'I couldn't get rid of him.'

I'm surprised she remembers. We won him together at the funfair at Portobello Beach when we were both nine, the summer it was baking hot for weeks and weeks, and Neil took time off to spend time together there, letting us hang out winning cheap cuddly toys at the hook-a-duck stand, and filling up on candy floss and sticky pink lollipops.

'Do you remember winning him?' I look at his grubby, lopsided bear face. He's sat on the shelf in here since Lauren went: not mine, not hers – but *ours*. Neither of us wanted to claim him.

'Yeah. Dad was with that woman from work. Do you remember, he was always taking us there that summer?'

'And Mum was always here, working.' I flick a glance in Lauren's direction, looking over the top of the oversized teddy, which she's now hugging, her arms wrapped tightly round him. It's occurred to me before, but I wonder if she's ever put two and two together . . .

'That woman from work –' Lauren sighs – 'there's been quite a lot of them in my life.'

'Do you think she was . . . ?'

'Oh God, yes.'

'Poor Mum.'

'Poor all of them, if you ask me.' Lauren sits down on the edge of the bed and places Blue Teddy on top of her pillow. 'I love him, because he's my dad, but he's . . .'

I raise my eyebrows and say, cautiously, 'A bit of a . . .'

'Dick.' Lauren says firmly.

We both laugh. It's nice, and it's taken me by surprise. It's as if Lauren's two people in some ways. The brittle, designer-clothes, scary one at school, and the same person she used to be when she lets her guard down.

'Nice to hear you two laughing,' shouts Mum through the banister.

I leave Lauren to get on with her unpacking. 'Just shout if you need anything,' I say over my shoulder, and head back down the stairs. My phone is burning a hole in my pocket. It's buzzed three times while I've been up there, but I didn't want to check it when she might see.

'I'm looking forward to getting this cast off,' says Mum.

She's become quite adept at managing her crutches, hanging her belongings in a little bag that hangs round her neck. She has a flask of coffee to keep her going, and I make sure she's got whatever she needs before I go out anywhere. It's been strange to feel so much freedom at a time when she's been tied to the sofa. All the time before when she was able to get around – but didn't – I felt like I couldn't leave the house, terrified she might not be OK. But now it feels like breaking her ankle has been the start of her new life.

'How long do you have to go?'

'I've got the fracture clinic coming up,' she says. 'I'm hoping they'll take this off and give me one of those walking boots.'

'Is that like one of those grey space-boot thingies?'

'You're too young to know what a moon boot is!' She laughs. 'Yes – exactly that. If I get one of those, I can actually get out, and I've got so much stuff to get on with. I can't wait.'

She's smiling again, and her face looks so much younger. Cressi came round and took her to the hairdresser, and now her hair is a bright shiny red. She's even wearing make-up. And earrings. I haven't seen her looking this much like her old self in so long.

She lowers her voice to an almost-whisper.

'Are you two girls going to be OK?'

I flick a glance towards the door, half expecting Lauren to appear, summoned because we're talking about her.

'She seems nicer than I expected.'

'She is nice,' Mum says, laughing. 'Why do you say that?'

'You don't go to school with her.' She wouldn't understand.

'No, but she's still the same Lauren. She might not live with us, but she's still part of our family.'

'Like Neil is?' I pull a face.

Mum makes a strange sort of snorting noise. 'Neil is a law unto his bloody self.'

I mime counting out a wodge of notes. 'Here you are, darlin' – buy yourself something nice.'

Mum snorts again, with laughter this time. 'Exactly.'

She pulls the laptop closer towards her and hitches it on to a cushion on her legs.

'Do you want anything?' I ask, balancing her crutches by the side of the sofa so they're easy to reach.

She shakes her head. 'I'm fine. So, what are you up to this afternoon? Are you helping Lauren unpack?'

'Not sure yet,' I say. If she hadn't broken her leg and I hadn't spent all my time before that worrying about her, I might have tried to sort out a proper summer-holiday job besides the swimming, but the weeks stretch out ahead of me, and there's nothing to fill them – well, nothing except –

I pull my phone out of my back pocket and type in the code to unlock it. I've got it set so messages don't even show on the screen . . . I'm not sure why. It's not as if I'm hiding anything from anyone.

Morning, beautiful!

I put a hand to my mouth, hiding a smile. My heart leaps.

'You OK, honey?' Mum looks up.

'Just a joke thing –'

Hope it goes OK with the wicked stepsister. Let me know what's happening.

Are you around later? X I type, and hold the phone for a second, hoping he'll reply.

While I wait, I decide to scroll through my phone, half wondering if Lauren's put up a snarky comment somewhere about having to spend half her summer holidays slumming it with us – but there's nothing. Nobody really uses Facebook any more. Social media only really works if you've got a social group to communicate with in the first place and, as I'm at the bottom of the heap, there aren't many people who've bothered to add me. I've got the friends who were on there from the end of primary school before everything changed, and a handful of distant relatives and cousins that live in Australia. But it's pretty much tumbleweed for me. I could look up Ed, but . . . I realize I don't even know his surname.

Edward . . . I type it in the search box, and a sea of anonymous faces appears on the screen – not one of them is him –

A message flashes across the screen.

Got to go and do family stuff this evening.

I feel a wave of disappointment for a second. All last week, Mum's been thinking I've been working at the pool, helping out with the swim school. I have – some of the time – but that's only in the mornings. The afternoons have been a blur of long walks in the woods, holding hands and talking and talking until we run out of words, and then kissing. I feel the same jolt of excitement running through me that I get every time we are together. It's like discovering a whole new life was waiting for me. All I had to do was dive into the water of the pool and bump into him and . . . It's not just the kissing. It's not just the way his eyebrows knit together or the way his face lights up in that huge smile when I climb off the bus. I feel like we're in that part of a film where it's all kissing and holding hands and everything's going right for once. And I think that's it. Everything is going right for once, and I like it.

Message me later then, I type.

I will.

Ed?

There's something about typing his name that makes me feel weird. Nice weird, not horrible. It feels like a secret.

His reply is instant.

Holly.

What are you doing right now?

Sitting on a plastic chair in the garden, throwing a half-chewed tennis ball for Meg. You?

Wondering if I should check and see how

Lauren's doing with her unpacking:-/

Uh-oh.

She's been quite . . . nice.

Body snatchers?

I laugh.

Mum looks up from her laptop. 'Is that Allie?'

I shake my head.

Got to go, Ed types. *A wild mother approaches.*

I send a heart emoji and a kiss. Three hearts pop back, one by one:

<3

<3

<3

I smile at my phone and slip it back into the pocket of my jeans. And I think fleetingly about Ed's mum, and I wonder when the subject's going to come up again. It feels like we've both got this *thing* and neither of us want to talk about it.

Lauren comes downstairs half an hour later. She perches on the edge of the chair under the window and chews on the inside of her lip, her brows gathered.

'I was thinking,' Mum says, closing the laptop with a decisive slam, 'that maybe we could do something nice for dinner later?'

'Pizza?' I say, thinking of the money Neil's left us, and the emptiness of the cupboards. There's a new place in town that delivers, so we've finally entered the twenty-first century.

'Why don't you girls make it?'

Lauren looks at me as if she's not sure how to react. I'm not sure what to do with this new, unsure version of her.

'Homemade pizza?'

'You used to love doing it when you were little.'

'We never do anything like that,' Lauren says. 'Clare's had a new kitchen fitted and she's completely paranoid about it getting messed up.'

'So you've got a kitchen that's not for cooking in?' I look at her, confused.

'That pretty much sums up our house.'

'Well, our kitchen's not exactly modern, but it's definitely designed for cooking. If I give you two some money, will you nip down to the shop?'

We've got herbs and olive oil, but we head off with a list of ingredients. The little corner shop on the estate has pretty much everything under the sun.

'Normal flour?' Lauren holds up a red package.

'Definitely not self-raising?'

She turns it over, reading the label. 'Definitely not.'

I hold up a tin. 'Shall we get pineapple?'

Lauren pulls a disgusted face. 'Pineapple on pizza is the work of the devil.'

'Is not.' I put the tin in the basket hanging over my arm.

'Is too.' She takes it out, teasing, and puts it back on the shelf.

'It's tropical.'

'It's rank, is what it is.' Lauren reaches across me, retrieves the tin from the shelf, and plops it back on top of the other ingredients. 'But if it makes you happy . . .'

We exchange a grin.

'Long time since we've seen the two of you in the shop,' says Margaret behind the counter. She's been there since the dawn of time, and knows everything and everyone. She's like a bible of gossip.

'Your da' still shacked up with that lassie from his work?'

Lauren nods.

'How's your mum's ankle doing?' Margaret tallies up the shopping on the till and takes the money from me.

'Getting better,' I say.

'No' seen her for what feels like months.'

I hold out my hand, and she counts out the change, giving me a handful of pound coins.

'Sorry, no fivers left.' Margaret purses her lips. 'Tell her I was asking after her.'

'I will,' I say.

Lauren lifts one of the bags off the counter, and I take the other one.

'*That lassie from his work,*' she echoes, after the door closes behind us. 'Her and a million others.'

We wander back up the path between the backs of gardens. The creosote smell of hot fences fills the air, and the sounds of children having a water fight in one of the gardens makes us laugh. Lauren squeals and jumps out of the way as a jet of water shoots over the top of a gate.

'D'you ever wonder what Fiona saw in him?'

'Frequently.'

'I mean he's my dad and everything, but . . .'

I pull a face that says, *Yes, I know*. It doesn't feel right to be too horrible about Neil when he's her dad, even if I personally think he's a complete arsehole.

'I think he's a good example of what not to look for in a relationship.'

Lauren laughs at that. 'You mean you're not after a sexist and totally unreconstructed 1980s throwback who genuinely thinks it's OK to judge women out of ten for looks and shag around behind his partner's back whilst spending all her money and living in her expensive house by the shore?'

'Um . . .' I say, as if I'm contemplating the possibility. 'That would be a no. Definitely not.'

'And that's why I'm steering clear of the boys at our school.' Lauren opens the back gate and holds it wide for me to pass through. 'They're all complete losers.'

As we unpack the stuff and follow Mum's instructions for making pizza dough, I watch Lauren unwinding a bit. Her hair's come loose at the front where she had it pinned up in tiny flower clips, and it's hanging down in her face. She's got flour on her nose, and splashes of tomato sauce up the front of her T-shirt.

Mum's sitting on the dining chair watching us and directing operations, and it reminds me of being little and learning to bake fairy cakes. Mum taught herself how to cook and bake, and she's really good at it, but for ages she's hardly done anything. Of course, when the house was a complete tip, it was pretty hard to cook anything, because the surfaces that are now sparkling clean were scattered with a mountain range of piles of paper and boxes and things. It feels like a different house – or like it used to when we were younger, only without Neil. Calmer. His whole act (and it feels like an act) is about being loud and making himself the centre of attention. I hadn't noticed before, or maybe Lauren's quieter than I remember. And she seems less prickly here, more like her old self. I wonder how I hadn't noticed before – she's in the popular set, she's always dressed perfectly and most of her best friends have hooked up with the equivalent boys from our year or the year above. But she's single.

'Is that OK?' She turns to Mum, showing her the rolled-out dough on a metal tray.

'Perfect.' Mum smiles. 'Pop it up there on the windowsill to rise for ten minutes, and while you're waiting you can clear up the mess.'

I throw Lauren the surface-cleaning spray, and she catches it with one hand.

'Impressive.'

'I've got skills,' she says, and when she smiles her nose crinkles up and she looks about ten again.

'Look at this,' Mum says, and beckons us over to the table. 'Cressi found it when we were clearing up. When *she* was clearing up.' Mum looks a bit uncomfortable. It's the great unspoken. Apart from the time when she mentioned the doctor and going for CBT, she hasn't said much, and I don't like to ask.

She's got a brown leather-covered album and she opens

it, revealing stiff board pages with photographs from a trip to Norfolk inside. I stretch over to the fridge and pull out the Coke we bought earlier, and Lauren reaches up, without thinking, and takes down three glasses. It's just like old times.

'Do you remember that boat trip?'

Mum points to me and Lauren on the front of her friend's boat. We're in matching pink shorts and blue T-shirts, our hair in bunches.

'Why on earth am I wearing pink?' I lean in and peer at the picture more closely. My hair was even redder than it is now, and my cheeks are flaming red with sunburn.

Lauren and Mum exchange a look. Lauren puffs a long strand of blonde hair out of her eyes, which falls straight back down again, landing on her still-flour-smeared nose.

'Don't you remember? You wanted to be twins. In fact –' Mum laughs – 'you insisted for the whole of the time we were down there that I told everyone you were.'

'Oh God.' I roll my eyes.

'We did!' Lauren nudges me with her elbow. 'And we spoke in that made-up language that neither of us could understand either.'

'Because twins can—'

'Finish each other's sentences.' Lauren clinks my Coke glass with hers and takes a sip, looking at me over the top of it as she turns the page. 'Oh my God, I forgot . . . !'

We all look down at the photo of a huge manor house with pink roses around the door.

'. . . Isn't that Joey Grey's house?'

Mum turns another page. 'Oh, and look at that! Do you two remember when we went to that pony-trekking place with Joey's kids?'

'Billy and Violet?' Lauren frowns.

'They're the ones.'

'They were in Allie's *Heat* magazine the other day, y'know.'

'For what?' Mum looks surprised.

I shrug. 'Kids of the Britpop gang, or something like that.'

Lauren looks impressed. 'Really?'

Allie had brought it up, thrusting the folded-over page at me while we were sharing a packet of chocolate biscuits (magazine and biscuits all pilfered from the shop, of course). She'd quizzed me, because she was fascinated by Mum's on-the-edge-of-famous past, but I'd shaken my head and acted like I could only just remember them. It was only eighteen months or so since we were last down there, when they'd paid for Mum to take me on a train journey that lasted almost the whole day.

When we'd got there, it was clear to everyone that she was a half-shadow of herself. She excused herself from the lazy, smoke-hazed after-dinner jams, where everyone would mess around by the river, floating in the little wooden boats or playing guitar and singing. I hadn't known what to do with myself, and Billy and Violet – who'd been like cousins to me – had changed. They were sharp-edged and London-ish and my life was unravelling, just like my clothes. We didn't have anything to say to each other. When I think of the difference between the awkward, stilted conversations we had that summer, and the way Ed and I run out of hours, not words . . . there's no comparison.

'Anyway, you can have that as a claim to fame,' Mum jokes. 'Tell the girls at school.'

'I already did,' Lauren says softly. She looks at Mum for a second. 'They know you were in a band.'

Mum's face registers a sort of shy pleasure. 'They do?'

I catch Lauren's eye and smile at her, and it's a genuine thank-you sort of smile. That means a lot to Mum.

The doorbell breaks the moment.

'You didn't order pizza by mistake?' I say, turning to Mum.

She shakes her head.

'It's probably Dad,' says Lauren, pushing herself up from the table. 'They've probably had another fight and the holiday's off.' She actually looks a bit downcast as she says that.

'I'll go,' I say. 'You get the pizza topping ready.'

I pull open the door and do a double take.

'Hi,' says Allie. She's dyed her hair bright pink and she's wearing a rainbow T-shirt and a denim pinafore dress.

I realize after a second that I'm standing there with my mouth hanging open. But I'm not the sort of person who has friends just turning up on the doorstep unannounced. The way we've lived until now hasn't really lent itself to that. And now things are different, but –

'We just thought we'd come and see what you were up to,' says Rio. He's in skinny black jeans, very polished black boots with pointy toes and a checked shirt. They both look like they've dressed up for something.

I keep a hand on the door so I'm hanging out of it holding it behind me.

'Also, we thought we'd better check in case you needed us,' Allie says, lowering her voice to a whisper, 'to rescue you from the clutches of the evil stepsister.'

'But I . . .' I stop and pull the door closed behind me, and they shuffle back on the front step to make room for me. We stand in a little huddle of three.

I'm aware my mouth is still hanging open. I close it and stand there for a long moment, looking at them, trying to think what to say.

Rio cracks his chewing gum and then looks at me, twisting his mouth sideways thoughtfully.

'Have we come at a bad time?'

'No.' I realize it's really great that they've come; it's just . . . complicated. I wasn't expecting it to be *nice* having Lauren staying.

I look at Allie in her rainbow outfit, standing there looking about nineteen and strangely confident (being outside of school suits her, I think), and at Rio, who has grown in a couple of weeks and is somehow almost as tall as me.

'How's it going at the gallery?' I sound like someone's mum.

'Ah.' Allie fiddles with the metal clip of her pinafore.

'That's the other reason we're here. D'you want to come with us tomorrow?'

'I'm working,' I say automatically. Not because I don't want to, but because I've spent so long saying no to things like that, it's just a habit. And I'm never going to have a life if I keep saying no to everything.

'Oh . . . actually –' I frown, hoping that I look like I'm just remembering – 'my mistake. I'm not.'

'Cool.' Allie nods. 'Be at mine for eight. Jack's picking me up.'

She looks a little bit pleased with herself as she says it. He's not Rio's dad any more; he's graduated to first-name terms.

'So anyway,' says Rio, pointing to the time on his phone, 'that's tomorrow sorted. Meanwhile we're supposed to be on a mission.'

I glance at the door without meaning to.

'I can't really —'

There's a shout from the kitchen.

'Honey, are you coming to do these pizzas? Lauren's waiting.'

Rio smiles. 'You'd better go. We'll see you in the morning.'

Mum calls again. 'Who is it?'

'Allie and Rio,' I say.

'Tell them they could always join us,' she shouts.

'It's fine,' I say, before they have a chance to say yes. I'm finding it weird enough that our house has an extra person in it, without trying to negotiate the social

162

weirdness that would ensue if I started trying to mix new friends with old family. I turn back to Allie. 'What time did you say?'

'Eight. On the dot,' she confirms. 'Jack doesn't like to be late because of the traffic.'

'Well, I'd better not keep Jack waiting,' I say, completely straight-faced.

Rio catches my eye, acknowledging the sarcasm behind the innocent tone, and grins. 'You'd better not keep Lauren waiting either,' he says, with an arch of his eyebrow. 'Happy families and all that.'

'It's not . . .' I begin.

But they've turned away and are walking down the path, Rio checking his phone, and Allie pulling her bright hair up into a ponytail.

The moment inside is lost too. We finish making the pizzas and eat them in the kitchen, but Lauren's looking at her phone, and Mum's reading a book, and afterwards I disappear to my room to message Ed, and nobody even notices.

I come back down hours later. Lauren's in the bath, and Mum's sitting on the sofa watching *Friends* and making brightly coloured crochet squares.

'I haven't seen you doing that in ages.' I pick one up and look at it. It's pink and green and white, with a dusty sort of blue around the outside.

'I haven't done it in ages.' She puts the crochet hook and wool down for a second and looks at me.

I pile up the four little squares she's made into a tower

163

and line up the balls of wool that are on the table so all their labels match.

'You OK?' She squeezes my knee.

'I'm fine.'

'I mean with . . .' She lifts her head, motioning towards the stairs. I know she means with Lauren being here.

'I thought she was going to be more . . .'

'Prickly?'

We share a secret grin.

'She's had a tough time too, y'know.'

I roll my eyes. I might be ready to accept that she's not one hundred per cent wicked stepsister, but I'm not completely on board with the idea that she's actually BFF-for-life material.

'Tell me about this Allie and Rio?'

'Oh, they're just people from school. They're nice.'

'You could have invited them in, you know. I mean now the house is . . .' She tails off again.

'I know. But it's awkward. With them, I mean.'

'Being in a three?'

I nod, my mouth set in a flat sort of line. I can feel it turning down at the ends. I don't want to go tomorrow for a million different reasons.

'You can only feel left out if you choose to let it in,' Mum says.

I give her a dubious look. 'Is that what your new counsellor says?'

She's been twice now. The first time, Cressi drove her. The second, she got the bus to the surgery, hopping up the

164

back path to the bus stop on Crawford Road. When she got back, she was exhausted, but she said she preferred to have some time to think things over afterwards.

'It's not, no. It's what *I* say.' She points to the poster in the hall that is in a frame. It's a black-and-white band photo of Mum, Joey and Anna. Tour dates are printed over the top of their faces, but when I look at it I can see that two of them are laughing, looking at each other and creasing up as if someone's said something hysterically funny. Mum's looking directly at the camera, her face solemn. I'd never really looked at it properly before.

'Those two were always like that,' she says, crossing her two fingers and holding them up. 'I was on the outside. I spent years feeling like it was something I'd done, or something I hadn't done. And I'm realizing something that I didn't hear enough when I was growing up, which is that – you're perfect just as you are . . .'

She lifts my chin with a finger, turning my face round to look into my eyes.

'I guess I haven't told you that often enough either.'

I give her an upside-down sort of smile, feeling a bit awkward.

'Thank you,' I say stiffly. She's still got a hand under my chin.

'Come here,' she says, and pulls me into a hug. 'Still enjoying the swimming?' she says into the top of my hair.

I nod.

'You seem to be getting a lot of hours up there. They're not overworking you, are they?'

I sit back.

'No, I'm covering some of the teachers that are away, that's all. The sooner I do my forty voluntary hours, the sooner I cover the cost of the training course – then I get paid.'

I'm lying, and hope she won't suddenly have a personality transplant and call to check up on me. But it's a miracle that she's even managed to catch a bus to the surgery down the road – the chances of her deciding to start making phone calls and investigating what I'm up to are pretty slim.

'They're not taking advantage of you?'

I think of Ed standing at the bus stop and the sensation of his hand curling under my hair as he pulls me into a kiss and the way the muscles of his shoulders feel when I wrap my arms around them, and I hide a smile.

'They are not taking *advantage*, no.'

The emphasis is lost on her. I give her a kiss and head back upstairs, my phone in my pocket.

Lauren emerges from the bathroom, pink-faced and wrapped in a towel. Her hair is dripping down her back.

'Hi, Holly.'

I smile and go to open my bedroom door, but she stops me.

'I've got something for you,' she says.

I turn back.

She takes a towel from the airing cupboard and bends

over, wrapping it round her head to soak up the water from her hair.

I wait.

'It's in here.' She heads for the bedroom and beckons me to follow her.

It's funny that she's already made the room feel like hers again – as if it's been waiting for her to come back and reclaim it. The house feels more like a home with three of us in it, instead of just me and Mum rattling around.

She pulls out a plastic bag from the drawer, and I notice her cheeks have gone even pinker – not just from the heat of the bath.

'I got this the other day when I was shopping.'

She pulls something out of the bag – it's black and expensive-looking. I can't quite work out if it's underwear or a top.

'It's nice,' I say politely. I lean closer, realizing as she's shaking it out that it's neither – it's a swimsuit.

'It's not for me.' She proffers the little plastic hanger with the suit attached. 'I had a voucher and I saw it and I thought maybe you'd like it.'

I take it from her. It's made of smooth black fabric, and instead of the sensible school-uniform Speedo costume I normally wear, this one is pretty with a scooped neck.

'I noticed yours was looking a bit dead when I took the washing out of the machine the other day, and . . .'

There's a moment where we both look at each other, and I know we're both thinking the same thing. I can't afford new stuff, and she's got loads of it.

'. . . Anyway,' she continues, picking up the bag and folding it in half, and then in half again, 'I hope it's OK. You don't have to keep it if you don't want to.'

I look down at it again and feel a huge grin spreading over my face.

'I love it.'

CHAPTER FOURTEEN

Wish you were up here.
Wish I wasn't going to Edinburgh.
Wish it was tomorrow.
Wish you were . . . I stop myself typing. What I want to say is *Kissing me. Now.*

I feel like I might be under a spell. I'm walking down to Allie's house, and it's so early in the morning that the only people on the road are exercise-fanatic joggers and cars heading up to Hopeburn to catch the train to Edinburgh. The city bus lumbers past, half-asleep commuters leaning against the windows, mouths hanging open. I walk and I message Ed, and I feel like I'm fizzing over with excitement.

'You're early.' Allie is clearly terrible in the mornings. She's swaying in the doorway, her pink hair standing up in fuzzy tufts, last night's foundation settled like a mask on her face. She rubs her eye and smears eyeliner and mascara halfway down her cheek.

'Morning,' I say. I shove my phone in my pocket and follow her inside.

Allie's mum looks up and smiles. 'Come in, my duck – you must be Holly.'

Their house joins on to the side of the shop, and I catch

a glimpse of her dad unpacking the papers and stacking them on the shelves.

'We're all running a bit late today. D'you want a cup of tea while you're waiting?'

Allie's house is dark and cosy, even in the middle of summer. The sitting room looks out over the Firth of Forth, and it's shabby and comfortable, not posh.

'I'll just be a minute,' says Allie, thumping up the stairs.

She must get ready faster than anyone I know. I've been up since six, had a bath, dried and straightened my hair, put on make-up to try and make myself look less like a twelve-year-old, and tried on and discarded about five different outfits. I pull the hem of my skirt down. It's shorter when I sit, and there seems to be an awful lot of thigh before my knees appear. I've got a grey cardigan and one of Mum's old band T-shirts on, and a jumble of plaited friendship bracelets tied to my wrist.

Allie's mum places a cup of tea in front of me. It's always awkward when you're sitting in a strange house. I clear my throat and press my knees together. She unwraps a packet of Kit Kats and offers me one.

'I may as well give you three these to take with you. Allie's refused a packed lunch every day she's been working at the gallery. I bet you've got one, haven't you?'

I look at her and pull a confused face. 'I haven't, no – but I didn't realize we were . . .'

I had some of the money Neil had given us shoved in the back of my purse, and a bottle of Coke in my bag that was left over from yesterday.

'Paying a fortune for Edinburgh lunches. I don't know what she's thinking of. Thank goodness she's got Rio there with her keeping her on the straight and narrow.'

I feel my eyes widening. Rio, the person obsessed with designer labels who dreams of living in LA and doing all his shopping at Whole Foods? He's not the first person I think of if I'm asked to picture someone with an economical nature.

'He's a lovely boy.' Allie's mum sits down beside me and unwraps a Kit Kat, snaps it in two and pops half in her mouth in one go.

She munches noisily for a second.

'Lovely boy,' she repeats, and looks at me knowingly.

I smile back, taking a sip of my tea.

'I can't help thinking –' she leans in closer and her voice drops – 'you know . . .' She gives a knowing sort of nod.

I look at her for a second as my brain processes what she's saying.

'Rio and . . . Allie?' I say.

She nods, slowly and emphatically.

I dart a look at the hall, hoping that Allie might come thundering down the stairs and rescue me from this conversation.

'I – I just . . . I'm not sure that . . .'

She rolls her eyes. 'Oh, don't start with that – I know, I know. Experimenting and all that stuff. I watched a programme on Channel Four all about it. But there's no smoke without fire, and the two of them are like –' she lifts her crossed fingers in the air, echoing the exact motion that Mum made last night – 'that.'

'OK,' I say.

There's a sharp rap at the door.

'That'll be Rio. Shall I get the door?' I say, jumping up so fast that I knock the tea off the table. 'Oh God, I'm so sorry.'

'Don't you worry,' Allie's mum says in her lovely Birmingham accent. 'Off you go. I'll sort it out.' And she gives me a massive wink as Allie walks into the room.

'What the hell was that about?'

Allie, Rio and I are crammed with a load of canvases in the back of Rio's dad's beaten-up old Land Rover. It's not the kind with luxury leather seats and onboard video – it's the kind that's held together with bolts, and rattles you so hard that you feel your brain coming loose.

We judder to a halt at the junction that takes us out of town.

'Your mother has decided –' I pause for a second and look from Allie to Rio – 'that you two are . . . a *thing*.'

Allie puts her hands to her face in a passable impression of Edvard Munch's *The Scream* painting.

Rio looks horrified. 'No way.'

I nod.

Allie looks at Rio, and the two of them burst out laughing.

'Never going to happen,' they say, at exactly the same time.

'I guessed that,' I say, and think about the fact that a

few weeks ago, before I knew them, I'd come to exactly the same wrong conclusion. 'But you might have some explaining to do when your mum's already heading to John Lewis to buy a wedding hat.'

We bump our way along the motorway, through the outskirts of town and into the centre of Edinburgh. I watch as the houses change from the low white-harling bungalows to the huge brick villas and the Georgian terraces of the New Town.

We pull up on the high street, under the bridge, and I look up at the buildings piled on top of each other and imagine the castle up there, out of sight, balanced on its outcrop of rock. It doesn't matter how many times I come here, I fall in love with it in a different way each visit. I love it here – the tourists that drive the locals crazy, the posh Morningside ladies with their little dogs, the half-drunk students lazing on the grass of the Meadows. It feels like everything you could ever want is here.

'Holls?'

Allie has been out to the Land Rover and has two canvases under her arms. Rio's stacking them neatly against the white-painted walls of the gallery.

'Sorry.'

'Can you give us a hand?' she says, looking at Jack for approval.

Rio's dad flashes me a quick grin, and his eyebrows dance upward in amusement as Allie marches back out.

'Allie's quite . . . keen.'

I smile. I feel a bit awkward standing there.

Rio's dad hands me a pile of printed programmes. 'I know you're not working – you're welcome to go off and do your own thing – but if you want to help me for a sec I could do with someone to just check these are all numbered.'

I check that there's a name and number printed on the front of each catalogue, and then when I'm done I skim through one of them, looking at the pictures that are shown inside.

'I'm hoping we'll get a few sales at this exhibition tonight.'

'Are your pictures in here?' I look down, wondering if I'd recognize which ones are his.

Jack gathers the catalogues up and puts them in a neat pile on top of the rough wood of the counter. It's made, I think, from scaffolding, the metal bars at each corner strung with lights, which frame the sign that hangs below it. This feels like the coolest part of town, and I feel like a scruffy small-town hick. Somehow Jack's faded, paint-smeared jeans and holey T-shirt look like they're a deliberate choice. I feel low rent and hokey. I pull my hands into the sleeves of my cardigan, aware that I'm taking up too much space.

After what feels like ages, Jack replies. It's like he's on a satellite delay.

'No – mine are going up after this lot come down.' He waves an arm at the stairs, where Rio and Allie are winding long pieces of metal cabling between some more scaffolding. 'That's why we've put them in the back room.'

Of course it is. We carried them all in – carefully, one by one – and placed them with pieces of hessian sack over the top. Millicent, the gallery owner, had laughed at Jack for his insistence on sustainable materials for protection, when bubble wrap would do.

'Do you want a hand?' I make my way to the bottom of the stairs and stand there, not quite sure what to do with my limbs. It's as if they've grown, and I'm Alice in Wonderland in here: huge and ungainly and sprouting, when everyone else seems small and neat and cool and thin – so, so thin. Millicent must be a size six – her waist is literally the size of one of my thighs.

Allie throws a staple gun to Rio. He catches it with one hand as if he's a cowboy gunslinger (which goes with his latest look, I can't help thinking) and turns to look at me, holding it as if he's planning to fire a round of staples in my direction. I step back.

'We're OK,' he says airily. 'We've got this.'

Allie nods. She's holding up a piece of wire with her arm and is sort of pinned to the wall. 'We'll be done in a bit.'

I amble around the gallery for a bit longer, trying not to look at the clock, hoping 'a bit' will be done soon and we can go out and do something.

Jack looks up from the huge Apple screen and clicks the mouse, closing down the page he was working on. I've admired every single thing on the walls, stood around trying to look casual, gazed out of the window humming a little tune to myself and I'm running out of ways to kill time

175

before Allie and Rio are free. I wish I'd stayed at home. Mum was heading to the hospital with Cressi, and they were going to Pizza Hut afterwards. My stomach rumbles at the thought, so loudly that Jack raises his eyebrows and laughs. I pick up one of the gallery brochures and flick it open, trying to arrange my face in an interested shape. At this point, I've read the brief descriptions of every picture so many times that I probably know the words off by heart.

'Those two have promised they'll sort the hanging rails this morning – they've got quite a bit still to do. Why don't you have a wander, come back for them in a couple of hours?'

I slip out through the glass door of the gallery and pause for a second, looking up and down the road. I can hear the rush and squeal of the brakes on the trains below as they pull into Waverley Station, and the distant sound of bagpipes blowing on the wind. The piper who stands busking every weekend at the top of Waverley Road makes a fortune, raking in the cash of delighted new-to-the-city tourists, who think that everyone in Scotland wanders around permanently in a kilt playing bagpipes.

The street is busy with tourists and locals and artists, bustling along – all with somewhere to go, except me. I step backwards as a long crocodile of schoolchildren, all dressed in jewel-bright T-shirts and chattering excitedly in a foreign language, swell and fill up the pavement. I press myself against the cool of the stone wall and watch them as they disappear off, marching in the direction of the Scottish Parliament building. Their tour guide holds a sign aloft, and their teacher, bringing up the rear, looks frazzled. She gives me a smile and says thanks as she passes.

I've got money for once. I could go shopping, or walk into town. But I don't – I head down the street to the old stone arches, which used to be used for storage and are now a line of expensive-looking cafes and arty shops and galleries.

The first cafe I come to has a little wooden table with two old-fashioned school chairs tucked underneath it, looking out through bright glass on to the street. I duck inside and stand for a moment, my eyes adjusting to the gloom at the back of the room.

'Take a seat,' says a voice.

I'm scrunching up my eyes, trying to work out where it's coming from, when a tall twenty-something guy unfolds himself from behind the counter. He looks completely at home here – hair tied back in a ponytail, a dark scribble of beard, a rough cotton apron tied round his waist.

'There's a menu on the table.'

I sit down and pull the chair in with a clatter of metal on concrete floor. The music in the background is soothing, sweet harmonizing voices with acoustic guitars. The whole place is so . . . together. It looks like someone took an Instagram-friendly cafe in Copenhagen and magically transported it here, to Edinburgh.

I pick up the menu and decide that for now I'm cool and laid back, and my name's not Holly but Mette, or something like that. I run a finger down the rough paper, trying to decide what to order. Even the menu is posh, typed with an old-fashioned typewriter, complete with mistakes, which are marked out with an X – but somehow it looks like that's how it's supposed to be.

'What'll it be?' He takes a pen from behind his ear and pulls a little brown notepad out of his apron pocket.

'Um . . .' I scan the menu again, rushing. I've been so busy soaking up the atmosphere, I've forgotten to think about what I want. 'A latte, please. And a – a cheese and ham panini. No, toast. Toast.'

I have no idea why I say this. But coffee and toast seems like the sort of thing to have here, even if, after he walks away, I look at the words typed in front of me and wonder what exactly an 'artisan loaf' is. I hope it's not something weird.

I pick up the menu and study it again, marvelling at the prices. We're right in the middle of the tourist trap, and it shows.

I connect to the cafe Wi-Fi – the rest of the internet seems to be on holiday abroad. My social media feeds are just full of sunglasses and sunhats, hot-dog-leg selfies, and photos of palm trees taken by people who are my friends online but have barely spoken a word to me since primary school.

'One latte,' he announces, placing it on the table in front of me.

It's in a hand-crafted pottery mug, and I pick it up and cradle it in both hands, watching as a family walk in and settle themselves at the long bench that runs along the wall.

The parents are both blond and healthy-looking, and they have an identikit boy child and girl child, both with tanned skin and the same mop of thick, luxuriant blond hair. The mother unhooks a tiny baby from the sling thing she has round her neck and curls it into her arm while placing an order. It's dark pink and has a shock of spiky dark hair and looks crumpled and fresh and new. The father catches me looking and smiles, his whole face lighting up. I duck my head with a tiny smile, but turn away, embarrassed.

I've always been fascinated by other people's families. I find myself thinking about Ed's mum as I wait for my toast to appear . . . It's been ages. Maybe artisan bread takes longer to cook, or he's gone to churn the butter by hand.

I haven't met Ed's mum, and he hasn't met mine. He hasn't met my friends, and I haven't met his. Our relationship exists in a weird sort of hinterland, in the woods and the trees and down by the canal, or walking round the castle loch talking and kissing for hours. My insides squirm slightly at that, thinking of standing in the shelter of the town hall doorway in the rain the other night, his hand pressed casually against the wall, me leaning back against the stone. We were talking, sharing stupid jokes, waiting for the bus to come, and not hurrying the kiss that we both knew was coming. As the bus rumbled into sight, he leaned forward, and I caught my hands round his neck and –

'Sorry.' There's a clink as the knife slides off the tray and on to the wooden table in front of me. He picks it up and places it back on the plate, stepping back as if to give me a moment to admire his artistry. There are two huge doorsteps of toast on a flat wooden platter, with pale yellow butter and sharp orange marmalade in little metal bowls alongside it. My stomach gives another growl.

I think about the booklet Mum brought home from counselling the other day and how it encouraged people to find mindful moments in the everyday. To stop myself from feeling awkward at sitting here in a cafe alone, I decide to focus on every little thing I'm doing. I listen to the sounds of the blond-haired children squabbling over a board game they've found on the shelf, and the whooshing of the coffee machine. I feel the anticipation and my mouth watering as I scoop out the sweet-bitter marmalade and spread it on the creamy butter. This mindfulness stuff is easy, I think, as I cut the toast in half and lift one piece to my mouth. It's like time slows down inside itself and every second lasts a minute.

I crunch down, tasting the sharpness of the bread and the citrus of the marmalade and –

My eyes, half focused, gazing out of the window, fix on a shape in the distance. It's a tall shape, and as it comes closer I watch as he raises a hand to rake those familiar unruly dark curls from his forehead, and at the same time I push my chair back from the table with a clatter and return the smile that lights up his face. I lift my arm to wave and his name forms on my lips.

'Ed –'

I'm leaning forward and his hand raises in greeting and –

My heart thuds so hard against my ribcage that I think it's going to burst out and crash to the floor.

I watch, silent, as a girl rushes into his arms, and he squeezes her tightly, so tightly that she lifts up – small and dainty, a handful of a person – into the air. And then a delivery van pulls up, obstructing my view.

The sweet harmonies coming through the speaker sound nauseating, and the tiny baby begins to cry a desperate, rasping wail, and I push the plate of toast away from me, uneaten.

The van pulls off, and they're gone.

I pay the bill, the server asking with a concerned expression if everything was OK with the food. I apologize and say I don't feel well all of a sudden, and he steps back as if worried he might catch my non-existent ailment, and I grab my bag and leave.

I crash through the door of the cafe and realize they're at the end of the street. Ed and the girl are facing each other, talking. She's gesticulating – an open-handed, helpless sort of motion – and I can feel my feet dragging me towards them even as my stomach feels like lead. I can't not watch.

As I get closer, I see Ed turn, letting out a shout of fury, and he punches the wooden gate beside them. The air is full of his anger.

And then he sees me.

His hand drops to one side, and his face turns a dark, awkward red.

'Ed,' says the girl. She looks at me for a second, her

brow creasing, and then reaches out a hand to his arm. He shakes it off.

He looks at me, and his face sort of crumples.

'Holly.' He says my name and looks at me, and I recognize the emotions written on his face – they're desperation and fear. I wish I didn't, but I know them both all too well.

I take a breath, readying myself to speak.

'I'm really sorry,' says the girl. 'Just give us a second.' She turns to look at Ed.

A group of tourists pause on the pavement, looking at us.

'I need to go,' she says. 'If they find out I've seen you, we'll both be in trouble.'

Ed looks from me to her. She gives me a helpless look, and lifts her hands in the air, as if to shrug, but apologetically.

'I'm sorry,' she repeats.

'*His* life hasn't changed.' I watch as Ed's hands ball into fists again and his face twists with fury. And he's shouting now. 'I was captain of the swimming team. I had friends. I went to a decent school. And now, because of him, we're left living in a shitty little house in the arsehole of nowhere.'

I feel like someone's thrown a bucket of cold water over me. The tourists are all watching now. One of them has taken the cover off their camera and they're taking photographs of my reaction. I take a step back, and he seems to remember I'm there.

'Holly . . .' he says again, but this time his voice is quiet.

I don't look at him. I stare at the pavement.

'Ed . . .' The girl reaches out again.

I look up – but this time he shakes his head, not looking at either of us, and spins on his heel. And we both stand there and watch as he starts to run, his long legs swallowing up the ground beneath his feet.

'He'll be OK,' she says.

I don't know what to say or who she is or what to do. I feel gangly and awkward, standing there, towering over her.

'I'm Claudia.'

I look at her blankly.

'Ed's cousin?'

I try to disguise the relief I feel that he's not furious at being caught cheating on me with someone else. That feels petty and trivial all of a sudden, now I realize there's something else – something bigger – going on here. But I can't believe what he just said. He seemed like he was totally down to earth, and all that time he's been cursing his father for forcing them to slum it out in the sticks where we live. I feel small, and cheap, and pointless.

Claudia quickly checks her phone, then stuffs it back into her jeans pocket. She pushes her long hair back over her shoulder. She looks . . . expensive. Like she wouldn't flinch at the cost of the stuff on the menu in the cafe. She gives me an apologetic smile.

'I'm Holly,' I manage to say.

She grins then, and I see the resemblance between

them. I realize she looks like him, only small and female and blonde.

'I know who you are.'

Five minutes later, I walk back along the road to the gallery.

'That was quick,' Jack says, looking up at me over the top of his black-rimmed glasses. He's sitting behind the desk, and rubs his chin thoughtfully, leaning back in his chair. 'You OK? You look a bit pale.'

'Just feeling a bit funny,' I say. 'I might sit down for a bit if that's OK?'

I curl myself up in the corner of the gallery, tucking my legs underneath me and sitting in the nest of leather cushions covered with a fluffy blanket. It's sunny outside, one of those bright blue Edinburgh days, but I feel my teeth chattering.

'Can I get you a glass of water?'

I nod gratefully and sit, gazing out of the window. Allie and Rio finish their work and escape in a clan of two to the shops, making sure I'm happy to be left there.

Jack passes me the water. 'Do you want me to call your mum?' Then he remembers. 'Oh, she can't come and get you in any case.'

'It's fine,' I say. 'Probably just something I ate.'

'If you're sure,' says Jack absently. He's got a lot of work to do, and he's returned his focus to the screen of the computer.

I pick up my phone and look at it, as if it can give me the answers.

I compose texts to Ed, then delete them. I can't think what to say.

Eventually the day ends, and with the Land Rover empty of art stuff, Jack suggests I sit up front with him, in case travelling makes me feel any worse. I tune out the excited babbling of Allie and Rio in the back, and gaze without seeing at the blur of the countryside as we make our way back to Kilmuir.

CHAPTER FIFTEEN

'Sorry you're feeling crappy,' Allie shouts as I climb out of the front seat of the Land Rover. 'Feel better.'

I manage to pull a *never mind* sort of face as I slam the door.

'Catch up on Sunday?' Rio calls through the open window.

I nod, and before I have a chance to say anything else, his dad has swung the car backwards and is heading back towards town. I lift my hand in a wave of farewell, but they're already looking away.

I have my keys in my hand, but the front door's slightly ajar. There's a pile of books on the side table in the hall that wasn't there when I left this morning.

'Mum?'

I shove my keys in my rucksack and hang it on the end of the banister before heading for the sitting room. I can hear music playing, and there's a smell of vanilla and spices in the air – almost as if she's been baking, except –

'Ta-dah,' she says, emerging from the kitchen door. She is beaming with happiness, and she lifts a leg in the air and waves it around.

I frown for a second, trying to work out what

she's doing, and then it hits me.

'Your leg.'

'I've been let out early for good behaviour,' Mum says, beckoning me into the kitchen.

I follow her and sit down at the table before looking around. My heart, which has been through more than enough already today, sinks.

'I'm making cinnamon rolls,' she says, and pulls her phone out of her back pocket. 'I found the recipe on Pinterest – look.'

I lean over and admire the picture.

'I've always fancied it. And now I'm able to get about – well, I'm not supposed to push it, but –'

She's talking fast and I scan the room, taking in the surfaces covered in flour and supermarket carrier bags, mixing bowls and pots of spices with their lids discarded. I feel the most awful sense of inevitability falling over my shoulders like a heavy cloak.

'You don't think maybe you should give yourself a chance to recover before you start shopping and baking?'

I think she hears the sour note in my voice. She cocks her head to one side and looks at me, her eyes thoughtful.

'I'm not "shopping and baking",' she says, picking up a bottle of kitchen cleaner and attacking the flour-covered surface. 'I'm making some cinnamon rolls for you and Lauren because I'm finally able to actually do something for myself for a change.'

I bite back the words I want to say. I've heard this before. When she was going to make our fortune selling

Avon cosmetics. When she ordered a load of crafting stuff and then it just sat gathering dust in bags in the hall until it was cleared away last month when her leg broke. All that ever happened was she got a burst of excitement about something, but then when it actually came to doing it she ran out like a clockwork toy that hadn't been wound up.

'Honey,' she says, and she puts the cloth down on the counter and comes and sits opposite me. 'What's up?'

I don't say, *This isn't fair – for the last few weeks I've felt like a normal person with a normal life and a normal house and I was almost thinking I could invite Ed back here and now . . .*

I just look at her, and I know my face doesn't say anything good.

'Have you had a bad day?'

I wave my head sideways in a non-committal manner.

She reaches forward to squeeze me on the knee.

'I'm not feeling great,' I say, and I stand up. 'I might just go and lie down for a bit.'

'Let me know if you need anything,' she says.

'I'll be fine. Probably just a bug.'

'Well, I'll come and check on you in a bit.' Mum's face brightens. 'Nice to be able to say that without it taking half an hour for me to bum-shuffle up the stairs, huh?'

The next morning, I catch the bus. There's an intensive swimming course on from ten until two, and Cressi needs my help.

I haven't texted Ed. I've composed a hundred different

messages, but I don't know what to say. And he hasn't texted me, so maybe he feels the same way.

After I messaged Cressi to say I could make it, I switched my phone off. I sit on the bus trying to work out how I feel. Apart from her – and Claudia, it turns out – nobody knows about us. I start to wonder if I made the whole thing up in my head.

I'm sure I didn't imagine him. I stare out of the bus window and begin to wonder if maybe I did. Or maybe he imagined me. I'm not sitting here getting butterflies in my stomach with the anticipation of him meeting me off the bus, and me wrapping my arms round his waist and kissing him hello. I'm feeling dread that he might be in town by some coincidence and I'll get off the bus and he'll be there and I haven't worked out what to say.

But he's not there.

Town is summer-holiday busy with gangs of halfway-through-the-holidays bored teenagers hanging around, out of money and out of inspiration for what to do, waiting for someone to come up with something. Even though I don't know any of them, I duck my head down and walk quickly, pulling my switched-off phone out of my pocket and pretending to look at it as protection. They might not be the people from school who make life hell, but they may as well be. A memory of Ed that first afternoon, dodging them exactly the same way I did, pops into my head, but I chase it away.

'Excellent. I was so glad to hear you were free today.' Cressi's sitting in the foyer of the pool, checking off a list of names on an iPad. She puts it down for a second and pulls a band out of her bag. 'We've got a lot of bodies around because it's the holidays, so the council have asked if my volunteers can wear these.'

I take the circle of fabric and look at it dubiously.

'Over the shoulder and round the waist,' Cressi explains, motioning across her body on a diagonal. 'Like a Miss World sash – that sort of thing.'

I raise my eyebrows, and she gives a bark of laughter. 'I know, I know.'

'Miss World?' I shake my head in disbelief.

'Just go with it.'

'Fine.'

The morning rushes past. The children are around four or five, and trying to get to a level of proficiency that'll take them up a level when the lessons start again after the holidays. I'm so busy that I don't have time to think about Ed, until I remember that I'm not thinking about him, and then Cressi asks why I look like a 'wet weekend'.

'It's nothing,' I say.

We usher the children into the arms of their parents. We've got an hour to grab something to eat and then half an hour of waiting before we can get back in the pool because of health and safety regulations.

Once the last child is handed over, skinny and dripping wet in their regulation swimming hat and school trunks, we unfasten the lane and allow the other swimmers access to the side of the pool we've been using. Moving the lane divider on to the side and hanging it up, Cressi gives me another searching look.

We sit down in the corner of the cafe with a baked potato each. I squirt mayonnaise on to my slightly limp-looking salad and tear open a little sachet of black pepper and sprinkle it precisely on top. When I look up, I realize Cressi is staring at me intently.

'Spit it out, then.'

I lift up my fork and rotate it.

'What's happened?'

'It's nothing,' I say again.

She snorts in disbelief. 'I've had you waltzing in here on cloud nine for the last however many weeks, and today you've come in looking like you've had all your happiness surgically extracted. What's he done?'

'What makes you think it's –' I stumble over the words.

'I know you think I'm some sort of ancient dinosaur, but I did actually have a life before I got married, you know.'

I put my fork down and tell her the whole story.

'. . . And I feel like – like I've turned into one of those people who meets a boy and stops having a life, and I feel completely pathetic.'

And used, and stupid, and humiliated, my inner voice adds, helpfully.

'You're sixteen, Holly.' Cressi attacks her baked potato with a knife and fork. 'This thing's like a bloody bullet,' she mutters under her breath.

'And?'

'Don't be so bloody hard on yourself.' She shoves in a

forkful and chews for a moment, before continuing with her mouth full. 'And everyone else, for that matter.'

I realize that I'm actually starving, and I'm once again reminded that I'm never going to be the sort of person who pines away through lack of food under any circumstance. I eat some of my lunch and think about what she's just said for a while.

'You're finding out who you are, and what the world is like,' Cressi continues, 'and that means you're going to balls things up.'

The cafe is baking hot, and the tables filled with gangs of children and their parents, and the sound of slushies being slurped, and the games machine beeping and whirring. My head feels full of too much stuff and I don't know what to do with any of it.

'And Ed?' I say bitterly, and I feel my stomach contract at the memory of his words. I feel shame. Shame at being poor, shame at living in a tiny little house, shame at coming from – what was it he called it? – *the arsehole of nowhere.* And, most of all, I feel angry at myself for feeling that way.

'Give him a chance,' she says, and links her hands behind her head, stretching upward with a sea-lion groan.

I keep my mind empty of everything as I help with the classes in the afternoon.

'You'll have your hours in no time at this rate,' Cressi says, taking a swig of water from the bottle she's stashed by the side of the pool.

I look down at the log she keeps. Once I reach thirty

hours of voluntary help, I'm eligible to go forward for Stage One instructor training. The pay's pretty good, and I'm hoping I can manage to juggle it with working on my Highers. That's assuming I pass my exams, of course. It's funny that everything that's gone on has pushed out my worries about the results. I'm concentrating so hard on not thinking about Ed, though, that it's as if all the other things I usually focus on have jostled back into position, and school and (lack of) social life and everything else are still there. They were just waiting quietly in the wings for the last few weeks, biding their time. I gnaw my thumbnail, tasting chlorine from the water. My skin is wrinkled and pruned from the long day standing in the pool.

We finish and hand over the children in the waiting area. I re-tie my hair in a ponytail and set off towards the changing rooms, but as I do a movement in the corner of my eye causes me to turn round. Cressi raises her eyebrows and motions towards the pool, where I see the distinctive, familiar sight – his face is underwater, but there's no mistaking the power of his freestyle strokes.

'Looks like you're not the only one who's taken to the water today.'

I turn on my heel and head for the showers. I'm about to pull my bag out of the locker when fury overtakes me and I realize that, no, I want to swim and this is ridiculous. I reach into the locker and pull out my goggles and swimming cap, pulling it down hard over my face so that – with the goggles in place – I'll just be another anonymous swimmer.

I hover by the edge of the changing room until he's at the far end of the pool and then plunge into the next lane. And in a second, the world is drowned out. I swim fast and turn my head to the right to breathe, just in case he happens to be looking my way when I take a breath. I count my strokes and settle into a rhythm, tumble turning and pushing off and one, two, three, four. My arms begin to ache – I'm a strong swimmer, but this pace is much quicker than I would normally go. I keep pushing on until I can feel my heart thumping hard in my ears and my muscles screaming at me to stop. I don't want to chance it, but I have to. I slow to a stop and hold on to the edge of the pool, keeping myself submerged so low that from a distance I must look like a bowling ball in black goggles.

And then I see him. He's standing by the wall beside the changing room, and Cressi is nodding at something he says. He shakes his head, pushing his wet hair out of his eyes, and turns away.

I swim slowly towards her.

'You planning on staying in there until someone gives you a medal?'

I haul myself out on my arms, sitting on the edge of the pool with my legs dangling in the water. My legs look whiter than ever.

Cressi squats down beside me, the whistle hanging round her neck. As she talks, she's still watching the pool area – she doesn't trust the newly qualified lifeguard we have on duty, and she's not doing a very good job of hiding the fact.

'Don't worry, I didn't tell him the tornado hurtling up and down the slow lane terrifying the weekend swimmers was you.' She indicates an elderly gentleman swimming a ponderous breaststroke at the end of my lane. 'But I did say that perhaps you two needed to have a chat.'

'You didn't say anything to him?'

'About what?'

And I don't know what to say – all I know is I realize that since yesterday I've had this creeping sense of shame. And a terror that she might say something, tell him what my house was like. If she lifted the lid on it, and all the clutter and mess and spiders and dirt got out, I feel like we'd never get them safely back inside. And I feel like it would spoil everything. Cressi's the only person who knows exactly how we lived.

'About . . .' I tail off. 'Nothing.'

'The two of you need your heads banging together. Get yourself changed. I'll tell him to wait for you in the cafe, if you like.'

Ed looks at me through his fringe as I approach and pockets his phone. 'You OK?' he says, and he doesn't try to kiss me.

I nod.

'Look, Mummy, it's Holly!'

There's a tug at my arm, and I look down to see one of the little girls, Sophie, from our lesson, her mouth stained blue with slushy. She gives me a beaming smile.

'She's my teacher, Mummy!'

I smile at the two of them, and Sophie, putting her

195

thumb in her mouth, potters off.

'She is adorable,' Ed says, smiling. 'They think you're amazing.'

I see another little boy at the counter with his mum – it's Christopher, and his mother has a habit of pinning me down after lessons to talk about his progress until I've lost the will to live.

I indicate the door with my head. 'Shall we go?'

Ed pushes himself up from the table, untangling his long legs from the chair with difficulty.

We walk, and don't talk.

We take a different path out of town, a way I've never been with him before. It's a road I know from childhood trips up here with Mum and Neil and Lauren, and it leads up the hill and into the farmland that takes us away from Hopetoun.

The pavement narrows and gives way to a single-track road, and we have to walk in single file, tall hedges on either side, the sound of tractors humming in the distant fields. There's no traffic to speak of – a couple of cyclists whizz past on road bikes, dressed in bright Lycra. A huge grey horse leans its head over a wooden gate, watching us as we pass.

'Are we walking to Glasgow?' Ed says, eventually.

'Nope.' I shake my head and look at him sideways. His mouth is curved upward in a half-smile.

'Are we going to talk?'

'Yes.' I nod. And then I see the sign for the footpath and say, 'It's down here.'

The path is narrow, and the earth baked dry. This has been the hottest summer holiday we've had in ages, and the whole place is heavy and buzzing with bees and sunshine. My limbs are aching now, from the walking and the swimming and the hours of standing in the pool. We trek up the path a bit further and down a little wooded path and – it's there.

'Wow,' says Ed.

I smile despite myself. We're in a tiny clearing beside a waterfall, which splashes into a pool filled with clear, peat-brown water and then trails off down a stream where the bed can be seen covered with stones. It looks like a picture-book scene.

'So,' he says, and he collapses on to the grass.

'So,' I say. I sit down and cross my legs and look at him.

He rolls over on to his stomach and puts his chin in his hand. 'I haven't been completely honest with you,' he begins.

My mouth dries as I try and form a reply. 'Ah,' I croak.

'But I think – I want to try and explain.'

I cross my arms as well as my legs, so I'm sitting on the grass like a pretzel.

'Go on.'

Ed rolls over again and sits up so he too is sitting cross-legged, facing me – or he would be, if I wasn't looking intently at a blade of grass about thirty centimetres to the left of my knee.

'I said I had family stuff to do yesterday.'

'Uh-huh.' I nod, still looking down.

'The girl you saw me with . . .'

I pick up a blade of grass, and tear it apart with my unbitten thumbnail.

'Claudia,' I say. 'Your cousin.'

He nods. 'You talked?'

'We did,' I say. I rest my elbows on my knees, and my chin on my folded hands.

'Go on . . .'

He looks at me, and I look back at him, and for a second we're sizing each other up, trying to work out what to say.

'She told me your dad isn't giving your mum any money and that she'd tried to help.'

Ed nods slowly. 'Something like that.'

I don't say that Claudia told me his dad – her uncle – has always given her the creeps because he's so charmingly, disarmingly nice. Or that I should ask Ed, because it wasn't her story to tell. I don't know how to say that. All I know is that it feels like there's a lot more to Ed's family than he's let on.

'My mum would kill me if she knew I'd met up with her. We're – well, it's difficult . . .' He screws up his face. 'I hate him.' His voice is flat. 'And I'm sorry that I ran.'

He looks down at the ground, and I can see a muscle twitching in his jawline.

'I was so angry.'

'It's OK,' I say, thinking of his red face and the way he ran, as if he wanted to escape from everything.

'And I didn't mean to be . . . I hurt your feelings.'

I feel the hot-shame feeling again.

'Look,' I begin. 'I know that you come from a completely different world. And I've never been captain of a posh school swimming team or lived in a huge house. So I don't know how it feels to go from that to living . . . the way we do.'

'It was a really horrible thing to say.' He looks down at the grass and pulls up a strand, tearing it down the middle. 'I didn't mean to hurt you.'

I think of the times when I've argued with Mum and when she threw a mug at the kitchen wall because she was tired and fed up of having no money and we couldn't pay the bills.

'It's OK.' I realize I keep saying the same thing, over and over.

'And I'm ashamed.' His voice is quiet.

'Of what?'

For a second, I think he means he was embarrassed to be seen with me.

'I'm no better than him, am I?'

I shake my head. 'That's not true.'

'I lost it and punched a gate. What's next?'

'Everyone loses their temper.'

'Not everyone hits their wife, though, do they?'

Ed spits the words out, pulling up a handful of grass and throwing it down. He lifts his eyes to meet mine. They're almost black.

'That's why we live here.'

And it all makes sense. Ed, with his expensive too-small clothes, and his posh public-school accent. He's not here because his mum wanted to downsize to a village and make jam.

'We don't see my dad – or his side of the family – any more. We can't.'

'Can't?'

Ed pushes his arms out for a second and stretches them out so I see how short his sleeves are, his wrists poking out of the ends. He indicates the hole in his jeans.

'We don't see my dad any more because we're living in a safe house.'

And his face goes red again, the same colour it did when he ran off. I realize that, for someone like him, this probably seems huge. To me, living on the edges of things, it's just another example of the way life is. It's not always perfect and shiny, even if it looks that way on the surface. I think about Lauren and her expensive clothes and designer schoolbag.

'It's only temporary,' he carries on. 'He's not allowed to come near us. And Mum's not supposed to go near him . . . not that she'd want to.' His big mouth is set in a flat line. He chews the inside of his cheek.

'You mean he's banned?'

'There's an order. Some sort of protection thing. I shouldn't have met up with Claudia – they'd say that was putting myself at risk.'

'But she doesn't like him,' I say, without thinking.

'I know. That's why I asked if she'd find out what was going on. I got her to listen in on my dad and hers talking. He's told everyone Mum's mentally ill and she's making it all up, says he's not paying any maintenance to her because she can't be trusted.'

'That's why you were so angry.'

'Yep.' He drops his gaze again. 'And look how I behaved.'

'You're not the same as him.'

And then the words tumble out.

'He abused her. It started with words. He used to make her cry, and he'd talk to her one way when people were around, and then when they left he'd be . . . vicious.'

His face is unreadable. The air is still and there's one blackbird singing in the trees above us and the moment hangs there and neither of us says anything.

'And I feel bad, because he used to talk to her like she was a piece of dirt. I grew up and I used to listen to him using her as a figure of fun. He'd mock her, and make her feel small. And, once I realized it was happening, I couldn't work out how to make him stop.'

I reach forward and pick up his hand, holding it in mine.

'It's not your job to make him stop.'

'And then one day something went wrong at work, and he was drinking wine and he hit her across the face. I heard a crash and came down from my room, and he tried to act like everything was OK.'

'And that's when you left?'

He shakes his head and almost smiles. 'You'd think.'

'What happened?'

'He apologized, said he'd see a counsellor, promised things would change. Mum wore make-up to cover the red hand print on her face.'

I feel sick thinking about it.

'Nothing did change, though,' Ed says. He turns my hand over and traces the lines on my palm for a moment before he continues, his voice quieter and lower. 'He got missed over for a thing at work and came home furious. He drank a bottle of red wine before dinner and spent the whole meal criticizing Mum's cooking and my schoolwork. Then he lost it, pushed her across the kitchen, and I got in the way. He went to hit me, but then he stopped himself.'

'And that's when you left?'

He nods.

'She picked herself up off the kitchen floor and we grabbed our stuff and went. He said we'd come crawling back the next day.'

'But you didn't.'

Ed shakes his head.

'They sorted us out a B&B place, and then they moved us to the house out here. It's only temporary, until Mum gets money sorted. But, meanwhile, he's got everything, and we've got nothing.'

He lifts his foot, indicating his holey trainer again.

'And where is he now? Did he get in trouble with the police?'

Ed laughs, but it's a hollow, angry sort of laugh. 'Well, he's not allowed near Mum, but he's not exactly suffering.'

He pushes himself up to standing and bends down, taking a handful of stones from the edge of the stream. He throws them into the pool so they splash in, one after the other.

'He's in our house in Edinburgh. With all our stuff. And all Mum's stuff too.'

'Can't you get it back?'

'It's complicated. He's . . . he says he'll give it back if I'll go and see him. He passed on the message through Claudia.'

He runs a hand through his hair, leaving a smudge of mud on his forehead.

'That must be . . .' I trail off. I think about the way Mum and I have lived and how, despite it all, there's always been love. And I wonder how it feels to have a dad who behaved like that, and I feel strangely glad that mine isn't in the picture at all.

'I thought perhaps if I went to see him, maybe I could make him see that the way he's behaving isn't OK.'

I don't know very much about situations like this, but I know that doesn't sound like a good idea.

'I thought you said you weren't allowed to?'

He shrugs. 'I'm not really. He doesn't know where we are. The women's refuge people helped. My grandpa sent some money. He doesn't really know what's going on. He's usually drunk on sherry by lunchtime.'

He squats back down beside me and looks at me directly.

'I thought if I met up with Claudia yesterday, maybe she could go and get our stuff back, or something.'

'And can she?'

'She's going to try.'

'But is she safe with him?'

He shakes his head. 'I think it's only Mum he had a problem with.'

I can feel the expression on my face shifting to a frown of confusion. If he's capable of hitting Ed's mum, surely he's capable of hitting another woman – especially someone who's trying to get one over on him?

'That's why all my stuff looks like this. We're waiting to get money sorted out, but he's making it as difficult as possible.'

'And you had to leave your school and all your friends and everything?'

Ed gives a wry sort of smile. 'That bit wasn't exactly the end of the world.' He topples over on his knees, and laughs for the first time that afternoon. It's nice to see the smile that stretches across his whole face and shoots his eyebrows upward into the thatch of his hair.

'Which school did you go to?'

He names one of the exclusive private schools in the poshest part of Edinburgh. No wonder he has the accent that he does.

'And now you're at Hopetoun High?' I scrunch up my nose.

Ed shrugs. 'School's shit wherever you are. At least here people make it clear they don't like you.'

'Why don't they like you?' I think about every time a gang of people our age has come past when we've been together, and how Ed has shrunk and tried to make himself invisible, just the same way I do in Kilmuir.

'Where'd you want to start? You know what it's like – if

you don't conform in every way, you're in trouble. Too tall, too posh, too many weird clothes with holes in . . .'

'But they're all –' I motion to the logo on the front of his T-shirt.

'Not the right label.' He laughs. 'Back in Edinburgh, I could wear this lot and blend into the background. Here I stick out like a sore thumb.'

'And your dad has all the money?'

'Literally. Everything we own.' A shadow passes over his face as he says it. 'Mum inherited the house from my granny. He's taken everything.'

'So why can't you throw him out?'

It doesn't make sense.

'Simple. He's incredibly powerful, he's incredibly well respected and, believe it or not, he's convinced everyone we used to know that Mum walked out on him because she's having an affair.'

'How do you know?'

'Claudia told me. He had everyone in the family round for dinner last week and did the whole poor-little-me act.'

'But that's not fair on your mum.'

Ed shrugs again. 'Nope.'

I think about her hurtling up the high street and the angry voice as she beckoned him into the car that first night we sat and talked by the canal.

'That's awful.'

He nods. 'That's why I'm going to get him back.' He sighs. 'I'm sorry for what I said, and for the way I behaved.'

'It's OK.'

And I realize it makes sense. When you're living half a life, desperately trying to hide what's going on at home, the stress feels like a mountain inside. I sometimes used to look at the people at school who seemed to have everything easy, with their two-car families and their nice summer holidays to France, and I'd feel twisted up with envy that their lives were so normal. I'm not surprised all those feelings burst out of us. I reach forward and tangle my fingers in his. And I say it again.

'It's OK.'

We sit in silence, listening to the splash of the waterfall and the birds in the trees overhead. Ed's fingers are laced in mine, and his head's in my lap, looking up at me, his long body sprawled out on the grass. And then somehow we're lying beside each other and his hands are tangled in my hair and I'm kissing his jaw where the muscle was jumping and he rolls on top of me so I'm pinned to the ground underneath his weight and I'm the best kind of breathless I've ever known and I realize that it's lucky we're somewhere we might get caught because I'm not sure either of us would stop – but there's a whistle in the trees somewhere as a walker calls their dog and we both roll on to our backs and look at the sky through the branches and burst out laughing.

'I've got a confession to make,' I say, reaching out and lacing my fingers through his. 'I thought Claudia was your secret Edinburgh girlfriend.'

Ed rolls on to his side and pushes my hair back from my face. 'No,' he says, and his big mouth curves into the smile

I love and his eyebrows rise slightly, and I know before he continues what he's going to say.

'In fact,' he begins, 'I kind of thought the position of girlfriend was taken.'

By the time we walk back, hand in hand, the sun has gone in. The air is thick and warm, but there are bruised purple clouds gathering over the edge of the hills. I swing Ed's hand as we make our way back to town. I'm sad for his mum that things are so awful, but I'm glad that Claudia isn't anything other than his cousin, and glad that something in my life is going right for once.

CHAPTER SIXTEEN

Lauren and Mum are baking in the kitchen when I get home. I try to ignore the fact that the hall has a heap of bags lying on the floor, and there are shoes and flip-flops pulled out of the shoe cupboard under the stairs. It's not my job, I remind myself, to stress out about the state of the house.

'Hello, honey.' Mum leans against the kitchen doorframe. 'Ooh, my leg is killing me.'

'I don't think you're supposed to be standing up on it for this long,' Lauren says with a laugh from inside the kitchen.

'You're probably right.' Mum flops down on the dining chair and pushes up the sleeve of her top. 'How was work?'

'Amazing!' I beam, thinking of afterwards and not the riot control of juggling handfuls of small children in a packed pool.

'Amazing?' Mum cocks her head. 'You're a bit enthusiastic for someone who's been out of the house since God knows what time this morning.'

I smile to myself. It's half seven, and I've been gone twelve hours. It feels like a lifetime ago that I headed for the bus stop, leaving the house silent.

*

A while later, Mum heads upstairs for a bath, and Lauren tidies up the kitchen. There's an awkward sort of silence.

'How's –' she begins.

'What –' I say at the same time.

We laugh and start again, both saying 'You first' at the same moment.

I sort of want to ask why she hasn't invited Madison and all her other friends up here. Madison lives at the bottom of the estate, so it's not like she's too posh to hang out here.

'Is Madison away or something?'

Lauren squeezes out the kitchen cloth and hangs it neatly on the tap to dry. She doesn't reply for a long moment.

'No, she's around . . . I think.'

And there's something in the way she says the words that suggests she wants me to ask.

'You *think*?'

'I'm trying to have a bit of a break from her. She's quite –'

There's a moment when we look at each other, and neither of us says anything. We don't need to.

'Your mum seems so much happier, don't you think?' Lauren lifts the kettle. 'D'you want tea?'

I nod.

'What were you going to say?' she asks, pulling out mugs from the cupboard and milk from the fridge.

'I dunno,' I say. 'Just . . .'

I pause. It's weird, because Lauren being here feels like it makes sense, and until now I've been on guard, waiting for her to bring the rest of her gang of friends around and make me feel like a social outcast. Now I realize she's avoiding them too.

The silence hangs in the air as the kettle rumbles to a boil.

I take my phone out and message Ed.

'Here you are,' Lauren says, sliding a cup of tea under my nose.

Ed's reply flashes up on the screen, and I feel her eyes on it, taking it in before I have a chance to stuff the phone back in my pocket and pick up the mug as if nothing's happened.

'Who's Ed?' Her mouth curves into a curious smile and she sits down opposite me, cupping her mug in her hands and looking at me over the top of it.

'Just a friend,' I say, and the words sound so unlikely that when she looks me directly in the eye and her eyebrows shoot up I give a tiny, self-conscious smile.

'A friend,' she says, teasing.

'Yep.'

'Do I know him?'

I think again of Madison's perfectly dressed gang at school and the way they sashay through the corridors as if they own the place. 'No.'

And then I think of Ed's expensive-but-too-small clothes and realize that maybe in another world he'd fit in with her far better than he does with me, and I feel a bit uncomfortable.

'He's just someone I met at the pool.'

'I thought you seemed a bit keen on spending as much time in Hopetoun as possible.'

'I happen to be a very dedicated member of staff,' I say, teasing.

'Of course.' Lauren laughs, and she seems so much like her old when-we-were-a-family self that it's lovely. She leans forward and whispers, 'Have you got a photo?'

I feel myself blushing. 'Of my friend, you mean?'

'Of your friend Ed, who is just a friend and definitely nothing else.'

'I might have.' I grin at her and scroll through the photos on my phone, selecting one where he's sitting on a bench hugging Meg, her tongue hanging out and her chocolate-drop eyes bright. I pass it over.

'Cute,' Lauren says. She peers in closer. 'Dog and friend, I mean.'

I go pinker. 'Do you think?'

I realize that I've never quite finalized the question of whether Ed is cute to me because I like him, or weird-looking like I thought right back at the moment when we first met. Because he's got those big questioning eyebrows and a huge smile that takes up half his face and that mop of scruffy curly hair that flops over his forehead and – I feel a squirling in my stomach and realize that I don't need someone else to tell me if he is or not, and it feels like a significant moment.

Lauren hands the phone back, and nods. 'Definitely.'

The phone slips in my hand, and the photo scrolls sideways to the next picture, which is a selfie of the two of us. I go to put the phone away and Lauren laughs.

'Go on, let me see,' she says.

I am so red by now that I suspect I could probably be seen from space. Even my hair feels hot.

I pass the phone back.

'That is adorable,' she says, looking at the picture of the two of us. It was taken by Ed, standing behind me, his mouth to my ear and his long arm outstretched. I'm cracking up with laughter because he's whispered something as he took the picture, and my eyes and nose are scrunched up and my head bent. He looks directly at the camera, deadpan.

'I'm glad you're happy,' Lauren says, and she really seems to mean it. There's a fleeting second when her face registers sadness, but she takes a drink of tea and it's gone, almost before I can work out if I imagined it or not. I don't feel like I can ask her, but it isn't hard to work out how she's feeling. I wouldn't want to go back to living with Neil and whatshername if I was her either.

I hear Mum singing from the bath, and we both laugh, and the moment is gone.

'Bloody hell!' Allie kicks at a mountain of nettles on the path ahead of us. 'The plants are taking over.'

Since the last time they took me up to the clearing, nature has reclaimed her space. The little path is looped with bramble cables and thickets of sticky willow, which

212

wrap around our legs and stick tiny bobbles to everything.

'This is hideous,' says Rio, flicking each little green dot off with an irritable movement.

'You're really not cut out for this eco-warrior lifestyle, are you?' Allie picks up a fallen branch and thwacks down some brambles so we can step over them without being torn to pieces by thorns.

'I keep hoping someone from a spacious New Town apartment is going to come along and announce I'm their child and we were swapped at birth.' Rio purses his lips. 'This is horrendous.'

I swear he's become even more fashion obsessed since they've been doing this summer job at the gallery. His hair has changed again, gelled into sharp red sideways spikes. If you had to pick which one of the three of us grew up in a sustainable eco-house with hippy artist parents, he'd be your last choice by a long shot.

'There.' Allie knocks the swing with the branch so it sways drunkenly back and forth. 'I'm not getting on that until we've shaken off the spiders that are probably lurking inside.'

Tall spires of rosebay willowherb are growing around the edges of the fallen logs where we sit, and—

'Oh, bollocks.'

Rio gives the wireless speaker a shake. Rusty water leaks out of it.

'Forgot to put this away the last time we were here.'

'Don't worry.' Allie grins. 'I can sing if you like.'

'You're all right,' Rio and I both say in unison.

'Mum's given us a six pack of Coke and some picnic stuff.' Allie starts pulling things out of her bag with a magician-like flourish.

We crack open a can each and sit back for a moment, taking in our old kingdom.

'Funny that we haven't been here in ages. It seems smaller, somehow.' Allie stands up and walks over to the tyre swing, giving it another shake and turning it upside down so the rainwater falls out of it. She clambers into the swing and dangles her legs, pushing herself back and forth.

I take a stalk of the pink rosebay and pull the flowers off, one by one, waiting for her to talk.

He loves me, he loves me not, I find myself chanting in my head.

He likes me, I concede.

I'm sixteen. I *like* him. I don't know enough about him to love him.

I have no idea how you know if you love someone, anyway.

I mean, I love Mum. I loved Granny. I love . . . I think about Neil and decide that, no – he might've been my stepdad for a handful of years – but, no, I definitely don't love him. I think of Lauren's face as she grinned at me over the dining table last night and remember us on that holiday in Norfolk and our matching outfits and the way that even when she was with the bitchy girls at school she'd always hold back, keep an eye out for me, check how Mum was doing . . . And I realize that actually, I guess I do love her. As a sort-of sister.

'I don't know how to tell you this, so I'm just going to say it,' Allie blurts, the words tumbling out in a rush.

I look up and drop the flowerless stem down on to the dirt beneath my feet.

'I met a girl.'

'Oh my God,' I say, and I jump up and go to hug her, but she's still wedged inside the tyre, so I sort of flail my arms at her, and she is beaming with happiness and her pink hair is fuzzing around her head like a happy angel halo.

'Have you told your mum?'

I think about the last time I saw Allie's mum and her utter conviction that if she played her cards right she'd be having Rio as a high-flying city boyfriend in the future.

Allie shakes her head. 'I'm trying to work out how to.'

'Oh God, Allie – I'm so pleased for you.'

Rio stands up from the log and saunters over, standing with his hands in his pockets. He looks pleased too. I realize he already knows.

'How did you? I mean where? Who?'

'She's working in the cafe next to the gallery.' Allie's cheeks turn pink, so they match her candy-floss hair.

'I've never drunk so much effing coffee.' Rio rolls his eyes.

'What did you expect me to do?' Allie laughs.

And we sprawl on the grass, and she tells me the girl is called Milly and she's eighteen and taking a gap year before she goes to uni in Edinburgh. And she's amazing and funny and clever and gorgeous and – Allie barely pauses for breath. I haven't seen her so happy or so animated in . . . well, ever.

'She can fly too,' Rio says with a sardonic tone in his voice.

Allie punches him in the arm.

'Sod off,' she says affectionately. And she looks at me and pulls her phone out and scrolls through her photos and shows me a picture of a dark-haired girl with beautiful eyes and a shy smile, sitting on a patch of grass, which I can see is in Princes Street Gardens. She's holding a daisy chain in her hands.

'I made that,' Allie says dreamily.

'See what I mean?' Rio widens his eyes and flares his nostrils in mock horror. 'She's so loved up, it's actually nauseating.'

'Thank God you're the voice of reason, Holls.' Rio drapes an arm over my shoulder. 'You're my only hope.'

'About that . . .' I begin.

CHAPTER SEVENTEEN

'One minute forty-four,' says Cressi, tapping the top of the stopwatch triumphantly.

Ed pulls himself out of the water and stands, dripping wet, in front of us. I'm on my break from teaching, and we're timing him because she's had a brainwave.

'You're faster than our fastest boy in that age group by three seconds.' Cressi types something into the iPad. 'So the question is . . .'

'Will I join the team?' Ed pulls off his goggles and rubs his eyes. There are circles on his skin where they've pressed in, and his hair is hanging in wet corkscrews.

'Will you?' Cressi looks at him. She's not someone that you can say no to easily, I've found, but it's taken ages to persuade Ed to even do a time trial.

'I don't know . . .' he begins, hesitatingly.

'Edward –' Cressi's deep voice echoes in the pool area so several people look up, wondering what's going on – 'you were captain of your team at Edinburgh Academy.'

'Yeah, but –'

She raises her eyebrows.

I know what the *but* is, because we've talked about it. If Ed signs up for the team, he might end up competing against his old school.

'OK.'

'Give me a high five,' says Cressi, holding both hands up in the air. 'Or is that a high ten?'

I catch Ed's eye, and we both laugh at her, and then with her, as she does a funny little victory dance by the side of the pool.

'What made you change your mind?'

We're sitting in the cafe eating chips afterwards. Ed puffs out his cheeks and exhales thoughtfully.

'Dunno. Well, I spoke to Mum – that helped.'

I'd finally met Ed's mum, Lucy, on the high street one afternoon after swimming. I'd been working, and he and she were on the way home from the supermarket when we bumped – literally – into each other. I had hesitated for a moment, not sure whether I was supposed to act as if I knew him or not, but Ed had beamed his huge smile, and she'd surprised me by echoing it, pushing her long dark hair back from her face and putting down her bags of shopping to shake my hand.

'I've heard a lot about you,' she said, surprising me. 'Lucy Jarvis. How d'you do?'

'Hello.' I smiled at her and shook her hand. She had a firm handshake and was dressed in a pair of faded jeans and a striped Breton top. And she was tall too, and normal shaped. I mean not like a Twiglet.

'You must come round for supper one evening. Ed, will you sort out a date?'

Ed had looked at me and grinned. 'I think we can arrange that.'

. . . I smile, remembering.

'So,' I say to Ed through a mouthful of potato, 'what did she say?'

'That it didn't matter what was happening between her and Dad – I was entitled to a life of my own, and I should stop hiding myself away.'

It sounded so like something my mum – well, the new, old version of herself – would say that I couldn't help smiling.

I stretch forward and pinch one of his chips.

'Oi!' He grins, nicking one of mine.

'Well, I'm glad.'

I think joining the swimming team is a good thing. I say that even though Cressi has asked me for ages if I will, but I've always put her off. The people seem nice enough, but I just don't have the confidence to stand up there on a platform and dive in with everyone watching. I feel like if I did I'd suddenly forget how to swim and end up sinking like one of the seven-year-olds I teach – there's one girl in particular who seems to have her memory wiped every time she comes out of class. Either that or her swimsuit's been weighted down with stones. But we'll get there, Cressi says, because there's no recorded history of people just not being able to swim in all her time teaching there.

'Thing is,' Ed continues, 'if this is my new life, I may as well take the bits I liked from the old life and add them together. Right?'

I tap one of my chips against his in a toast. 'Right.'

The lazy days of the holiday are speeding past now. The shops on the high street are full of back-to-school stationery offers, and when I get up in the morning there's a sharpness to the air that smells like autumn. Summer doesn't last long here – by the time the Edinburgh Festival is over, the skies are darkening and we're reaching for our winter clothes, if we've ever cast them off in the first place. But this has been a strange, hot sort of summer, like nothing I can remember. Mum says it's reminiscent of one when she was a little girl, back in the 1970s. All I know is I don't want it to end.

Lauren's hanging out with the girls from school, and I'm heading to Hopetoun. I watch them walking down the road as I wait for the bus to turn up. It turns out that Amelie and Freya, the two girls she spends most of her time with, are nicer than I expected. They're never going to be kindred spirits exactly, but I'm allowing myself to hope that maybe – just maybe – this year at school might be OK. I hope I'm not kidding myself.

'Sorry about the mess,' Ed's mum says, opening the door. I'm flattened by an excited Meg, who lollops down the hall, barking with delight.

I look inside the little cottage and can't see anything but some piles of boxes, flattened out and waiting to be taken to the recycling centre.

'It's fine.'

I think about the fact that Ed still has no idea what our

house was like – and could be again, I suppose. I don't know how long Mum is going to stay well, and how long the house will stay the way it is. It gives me a nervous feeling inside thinking about it, and I'm glad that Lucy speaks and breaks the silence.

'Ed, are you coming?'

He thunders down the stairs, taking them two at a time.

'Come in!' Ed's mum beckons me inside. 'Don't stand there in the doorway.'

She steps back and welcomes me in with a wave of her arm. In the kitchen, there's a round pine table and four chairs, and that's it. The room is bare and pretty tattered-looking.

'I'm going to paint it white –' she motions to the awful green-flowered wallpaper – 'and get some nice gingham curtains.'

'Things must be getting back to some sort of normality,' Ed teases, 'because she's started obsessing over paint charts.'

'Watch it, you.'

She gives him a shove, and he leans down to give her a kiss on the cheek.

'We're going to get the train into Edinburgh, Mum.'

Lucy's eyes widen in surprise, and she stiffens, sitting up straight. She puts both hands flat on the table as if she's bracing herself.

'Where?'

'Porty Beach.'

She sags slightly. 'And not town?'

'Definitely not town . . . Are you ready?' He smiles at me and holds out a hand.

I feel slightly shy about holding his hand in front of Lucy, but I do it anyway.

'We won't be really late,' I say. I've told Mum and Lauren I'll be back in time for dinner – Neil's back tomorrow, and we're ordering a curry to celebrate.

'As long as you let me know when you've got there.' Lucy pulls out her phone and looks at the screen. 'I'll make sure this is charged.'

'Mum, I'm over six foot tall!' Ed laughs. 'Big enough to look after myself.'

She pulls a disbelieving face and then – clearly trying to convince herself we'll be OK – shoos us out of the room.

'I'll have the sitting room sorted by the time you get back. And we can sort out that bloody flat-pack shelf thing.'

'Deal.'

They've moved out of the little shared flat that was provided by the women's refuge place and into a tiny stone cottage with a garden that backs on to the canal. It's so small that all three of us have to duck our heads to get out of the door, and we wave as Lucy stands there, trying her best to look as if she's waving us off happily, but biting her lip as she does so. She pulls at a waist-high yellow weed that's growing by the door and lifts it up, pulling a face.

'Don't worry about me; I'll be so busy sorting this place out I won't even know you're gone.'

We walk to the station hand in hand. I see a couple of people I recognize from school on the other side of the road, and one of them does a double take, realizing I'm with someone they don't know. I smile to myself and carry on walking without even acknowledging them.

'She'll be fine,' I say as we sit on the metal benches waiting for the train to arrive.

'I know.'

'I spent so long worrying about Mum. I know what it feels like, though.'

Ed squeezes my hand. 'She's still frightened of him.'

'I'm not surprised.'

The train squeals to a grinding halt in front of us, and we wait for the flocks of tourists to make their way out of the doors before climbing on, taking two seats side by side. I lift the arm rest and shuffle sideways so our sides touch. I turn to look at Ed's profile. He's gazing out of the window, but his eyes are glazed and unfocused as we pull away from the station towards Edinburgh.

'Oreo for your thoughts?'

'I was just thinking that it was really shitty that Mum's got to try and make that place look nice when we've got all that stuff at home.' He stops himself. 'Not home. What was home?'

I think about the little cottage and how sweet it looked, with the garden backing on to the canal path. It looked like a dream house to me – and I knew that if Mum could see it she'd say the same thing. Our house backs on to the road that circles the town, with lorries and buses passing by as they avoid traffic and take the rat run to the industrial estate.

'What was it like?' I almost don't want to ask. Right now, Ed – with his scruffy clothes and his history wiped – feels like he's part of my world.

'Oh –' he screws up his face in thought – 'I dunno. You know how you don't really think about your house if you've always lived there?'

I think about our little white harling-covered house and the feeling of the stones on my palm as I stand outside. And the way that everyone on our estate has one of three different houses, so you can go inside and know where the bathroom is without having to be shown, and nobody has a posh garden, because they've all got the same rough creosoted wooden fencing, and the way the pavements meander between the houses and how we used to have roller-skate races round the block in the summertime.

'Sort of, yes.'

And I try to suppress the thought I have: that this train is taking us somewhere I don't want to go. Not to a place, but to a feeling. I let Ed's fingers lace through mine, and feel the coolness of his palm against my skin, and I sit on the train in silence.

When the train pulls into Haymarket, Ed turns to me and asks if I'm OK.

'Just thinking.'

'Me too.'

'Oreo?'

He lifts my hand and looks at our interlaced fingers for a moment.

'I'm pissed off.'

224

And I notice his brows are sitting low and knitted together, and his jaw is set.

'He's got everything and it's not fair.'

The train pulls off.

I squeeze his hand. 'But you said she's doing better.'

I think of Neil, and how long Mum spent in a pit of anger and depression, hating the hand that life had dealt, but not knowing how to get out of it. Now she was climbing out, making her way back into the world. And Lucy had her own place thanks to a savings bond she'd cashed in to pay the deposit. And when the divorce stuff was settled, she'd have more. I tried not to think about what that might mean. A tiny knot of doubt settled in my stomach – one that said that once they'd sorted everything out maybe I wouldn't be the sort of person Lucy wanted her son hanging around with. Maybe Ed wouldn't want me hanging around either.

'She is. But it just pisses me off.'

I've never seen this side of him before. Normally Ed finds the bright side, is the one who cheered his mum along as they found their feet in Hopetoun and moved their meagre belongings to the cottage.

I don't have the tools to deal with it.

The train carriage darkens as we roll into the tunnel approaching Waverley Station. I don't know what to say to make everything OK. As the train stops, Ed shakes his head and seems to shake off the mood that had taken over him.

'Sorry.'

'It's OK,' I say, and we head out into the noise of the station.

'If we head up here, we can get the bus to Porty.'

We walk up the hill, past the ever-present bagpiper, and on to Princes Street. It's only been a couple of weeks since I was here, and already the festival tourists are flocking around.

'Follow me,' Ed says firmly, holding my hand and marching purposefully along the street. 'There's only one way to cope with Edinburgh in August.'

He holds his arm up in the air as if he's a tour guide, dodging through the slow-moving tourists like a native – which of course he is.

'Excuse me, coming through!' He raises his voice commandingly.

I find myself laughing out loud as we hurtle along the street, and he stops suddenly at the foot of a statue, turning round and kissing me, pushing my hair out of my face with one hand and pulling me close so our bodies are pressed together. A group of language-school students giggle, and one of them does a wolf whistle and shouts something at us in Spanish. Ed laughs, his mouth close to mine.

'What did he say?'

'He bets that kissing the beautiful red-haired girl,' Ed translates, 'is more fun than learning about Scottish history.'

CHAPTER EIGHTEEN

We sit on the groynes at Portobello Beach and eat ice creams, and watch children darting back and forth, jumping the waves. I can sense that Ed's feeling agitated about something. He stands up and puts his hands in the small of his back, arching his spine in a stretch. Nobody knows us here. We should be having the time of our lives. But he's fidgeting, picking up handfuls of shells and jiggling them around, drumming his fingers on the side of his leg.

'Are you going to tell me what you're thinking?'

His face darkens for a moment. 'I can, but I don't think you'll like it.'

'Try me.'

'What would you say if I said I wanted to get the bus up to my old house?'

I feel my stomach dropping through my feet like a stone. 'What for?'

He flicks a glance at me from under his fringe. 'I just want to . . .' He pauses for a long moment before the words come out in a rush. 'It's Thursday, right? My dad will be working. If we go now, he won't be around.'

The feeling of dread is swapped for one of gnawing

anxiety. I'm not really known for my sense of adventure, or for breaking the rules. And –

'But you promised your mum we were coming here and not going into town.'

Ed's eyebrows jump up slightly. 'And you told *your* mum you were spending the day with Allie and Rio at the gallery.'

'Yeah, but . . .' I haven't got a leg to stand on.

I feel sick with anticipation and nerves as we sit on the bus for what feels like forever. Ed points out places he used to go when he was little, and I try to join in, but he's an Edinburgh boy, and our trips here were pretty infrequent. I don't have memories of weekend cinema visits or school trips to the museum. We came to the castle one summer with Neil on a work trip – one I realized afterwards was just an excuse for him to spend time with Clare. Lauren and I had trailed behind the two of them while they supposedly checked out some offices. We'd sat on a wall eating ice lollies in the rain while they disappeared inside for what felt like ages.

Eventually Ed shoulders me gently and pushes the button on the pole beside our seat. 'This is us.'

We're on the high street, just up from the Meadows where Allie likes to sit and pretend to be a student. Next year, she'll be up here with Milly, hanging out with a group of Edinburgh friends. Maybe we could all meet up, I think, trying to work out if Ed would get on with her and Rio.

We sway down the stairs of the double-decker bus and land in another world. Morningside is the poshest part of

Edinburgh I've ever been to. We duck down an alleyway, and Ed pulls his hood up over his head. The sun's gone in, and the sky is darkening with the threat of rain.

'It's just down here.' He's walking fast, still holding my hand.

And then we turn the corner on to a street where the houses are set back from the pavement in their own gardens, fences high to keep the world out.

We cross the road, and Ed peers over a stone wall and through a hedge.

'Nobody in!'

He sounds triumphant, but I feel sick with nerves. He punches a code into the box in the wall and the metal gates swing open.

We're standing on a gravelled driveway, which is big enough for about ten cars. It sweeps round in an arc, edged with grass that looks like it's been trimmed with nail scissors. In the middle of the lawn, there's a circle of purple lavender bushes. It looks like a park.

I hesitate. 'Do you think this is a good idea?'

'There's nobody here. It's fine.'

Ed strides forward and I follow behind, checking over my shoulders. I half expect a security guard to leap out of the bushes.

Ed's fiddling with a metal case that is hidden in a bush outside the door. It's got a number dial like a bike lock, and he frowns for a second as he turns the last one and pulls. The front of the box springs open and he takes a set of keys from inside.

'You've got keys *outside* your house?'

He looks awkward for a moment. 'For the cleaner,' he says, and pulls a face.

As I'm digesting this information, he swings the huge blue-painted front door open and it becomes clear that we really do come from different worlds. The hall – with gleaming black and white tiles on the floor – is bigger than our sitting room at home.

'OK,' I say, following him into the kitchen. 'So what exactly are we doing here?'

Ed looks around, running a hand along the smooth marble of the work surface. 'Well, this is weird.'

I can see now why the pretty cottage, which seems like a dream house to me, is – well, it's a step down to them. And I feel like a step down too, standing in a pair of faded cut-off jeans, with my hair in a messy plait down my back. This sort of place is meant for the kind of sleek-haired private-school girls Ed probably used to spend time with. I feel the knot in my stomach growing bigger and more uncomfortable.

'I just wanted to get something.'

'What?'

'Wait here.' He holds up a finger for a moment and shoots out of the kitchen, leaving me standing there.

It's like something from one of the house magazines Mum loves. She would be in heaven here – it's even got one of those big Aga cookers in the same shiny bright blue as the front door. It doesn't look like anyone has ever cooked here. The entire place is clinical and spotless and . . .

I feel myself shiver as if someone's walked over my grave.

I step out into the hall and stand beside a glossy wooden table, which has a huge floral arrangement in a vase. The smell of lilies is almost sickly sweet, and I step away, looking up the stairs, trying to work out if I should call Ed, wondering where he's gone. For all I know, there's an alarm or CCTV. I wonder if he's even thought of that – then I remember that it's his house, and we're technically not breaking in, even if it feels like it.

He runs down the stairs two at a time, a grin spread across his face.

'Sorted.'

For a moment I wonder if he's done something awful like thrown a tin of paint across the walls or smashed up the furniture.

'What's sorted?'

I spin round to look at him. He's rummaging in a drawer and scribbling a note on a piece of paper.

'Just a minute.'

He signs it with a flourish and leaves the pen and the note lying there, one tiny thing out of place in the immaculate room.

We slip outside, he puts the key back in the safety box and spins the dials, and we scrunch down the drive and out. It's starting to rain now, big fat splashes, which splatter on the pavement around us.

'What have you done?'

'Come on,' he says, and we run along the road and duck back down the alleyway and dart between the Morningside

Road traffic and throw ourselves on to the number 16 bus with half a second to spare.

We get the best seat on the double-decker – the top deck, right above the driver's seat. Sitting at the front of the bus, looking out over the city as we head towards the centre of town, it takes us both a minute to stop panting.

'OK.' I turn to him. 'Are you going to tell me what crime I've just been an accessory to?'

Ed puts his hand in the pocket of his hoody and pulls out a tangle of expensive-looking jewellery.

'When we left, Mum left all this behind.'

'Are you going to sell it?' I think of the trip I made with Cressi, when we took a heap of boxes of Mum's random purchases to the Cash Generator store and returned home with enough money to pay off the bills that were outstanding.

'It was from my grandma.' Ed shakes his head. 'I mean, she might want to, but I can't imagine it.'

'She didn't have time to take it when you left?'

'It wasn't really like that.' His face clouds over. 'When it happened, we literally grabbed a bag each and went.'

'So that's the first time you've been back there since?'

He nods. 'Pretty weird.'

'Yeah,' I say, and we sit in silence for a while as the bus makes its way down the hill towards Lothian Road.

I think about Mum and her posh musician friends in Norfolk, and how visiting there always felt a bit like being second best, and how standing in the glossy affluence of Morningside had somehow brought up that same feeling of not being quite good enough, and I wonder if Ed is thinking the same thing.

'I'm sorry our day trip to the beach turned into a heist,' Ed says as we walk down the high street from the station. 'D'you want to come back to mine? I'm sure Mum would love to see you.'

His manners are impeccable as always, but somehow tonight they make me feel uncomfortable, not charmed. I feel like I've seen another side to him, and I don't know where I fit in.

'I better go,' I say, checking my phone. 'We've got Lauren's last night.'

'I'll wait with you.'

We stop at the bus stop and sit down on the plastic bench where he shared chips with me that first night we met.

I shake my head. 'It's OK,' I say. 'I feel a bit freaked out at the idea you've got . . . that –' I stare meaningfully at the pocket of his hoody, which is bulging with jewels worth God knows how much – 'in there.'

'Good point.'

I don't get up from the bench but incline my face up to his as he leans over, his legs on either side of mine, and kisses me goodbye. I watch him striding down the street and feel unaccountably sad. There's a chill of autumn in the air. Lauren's going home, summer's almost over and it feels like it's the beginning of endings.

CHAPTER NINETEEN

Neil returns from his holiday with a tan that looks like his skin is made of leather, and arrives at the door with a bag of duty-free perfume nobody will ever wear. He's bought three bottles of exactly the same stuff.

'It's classy – Clare wears it.'

Lauren catches my eye, and our deadpan expressions match.

'That's very kind of you, Neil,' Mum says, putting the bag down on the kitchen table.

'Do you want some coffee, Dad?' Lauren goes to fill the kettle.

'You're all right, princess. I'm sure you're dying to get back to your own room, settle yourself back in and all that.' He jingles the keys in his hand.

'About that,' Mum says, and she gives him one of those looks. 'Can I have a word?'

And she takes him through to the sitting room, still limping a bit on her sore ankle, and Lauren and I stand in the kitchen and look at each other.

'D'you reckon he'll go for it?' I twirl a lock of hair round my finger and let it go, watching it bounce. Lauren's curled my hair with her straighteners so instead of being an orange mass of fuzz, it's hanging in fat, bouncy waves. I feel like a ginger Kate Middleton, only without the castle or the . . . I pause for a second, remembering Ed's enormous house and the immaculate gravelled driveway, and I laugh.

'What is it?'

'Just thinking about how weird this summer's been.'

Lauren gives a shy smile. I'm surprised how things have worked out with her. I suppose she's just another surprise in a summer holiday that's been full of them.

We stand in the kitchen and listen to the low rumble of Neil's voice and Mum explaining that Lauren wants to spend time with us, living here, and that we're part of her family, and she's welcome to stay as much as she wants. And neither of us say a word. We just listen in silence.

Eventually Neil comes back through, and Mum follows behind him, giving a grin and a thumbs-up behind his back.

'Well, girls,' Neil says. 'This has been a bit of a shock to the system. I have to say I expected to get back and find you standing at the front door with your bag packed, Lauren.'

'I think we've muddled along pretty well.' Mum looks proud of herself.

Three weeks ago when Lauren walked in the door and I felt sick with nerves at how it was going to work out, I had no idea we'd be here now.

'So you're not wanting to come back tonight?' Neil rubs his chin and looks confused.

Lauren darts me a look. 'We've got some stuff to do.'

He shakes his head as if he can't quite believe it. Neil's

not used to hearing people say no – he's a salesman, and his entire life is predicated on his staying put until someone gives in and does what he wants. It's weird watching him – he doesn't quite know what to do with himself.

'I'm not saying I'm not coming back, Dad.' Lauren puts a conciliatory arm round his waist and hugs him so his face brightens. 'Just that we're going to Edinburgh tomorrow. And I might as well go from here as from the other side of town.'

He shrugs. 'Fair enough, I suppose. Clare will be disappointed, mind you.'

Mum, Lauren and I all raise our eyebrows in a perfectly synchronized motion.

'I'm sure she'll survive,' says Mum, seeing him out.

The idea of Clare, who treats everyone under the age of twenty as if they're toxic waste, actually being disappointed that Lauren wasn't going back to steal her mascara and leave hairs in the bathroom basin was pretty unlikely. Lauren had sat one evening telling us just how clear Clare had made it that she wasn't welcome there. She wasn't allowed to eat anything without asking permission. Eyebrows were raised if she was in the bathroom for too long. And Clare's dog, Alfie, was a no-go area.

'She's actually told me that I'm not to tell anyone he's my dog.'

'That's insane,' Mum had said.

'I know. But I think she can't bear sharing Dad, and this is her way of making up for it.'

'Families can be pretty weird,' I'd said. And we'd gone out to the back door and picked dandelions from the roadside and fed them to Courtney Love, and I'd found myself telling Lauren that she could share our rabbit any time she wanted. It sounded strangely childish, but at the same time the delight on her face suggested that maybe it was exactly what she'd needed to hear.

Families *can* be pretty weird. Neil drives off in his gleaming Range Rover, and Mum and Lauren wash up the dishes from lunch. I fish my schoolbag out from the cupboard under the stairs and put my festering PE kit in the washing machine.

'I can't face going back,' Lauren says. She's biting her lip.

'We'll be fine.'

I straighten up and do a little finger dance to cheer her up, singing the 'I'll Be There for You' theme tune from the beginning of *Friends*. It makes her laugh, and I feel genuinely, uncomplicatedly happy. It's a good feeling.

Thursday, though, will be the real test. I'm throwing myself in at the deep end and taking Lauren and Ed on the train to Edinburgh. We're going to head up to the gallery, meet up with Allie and Rio, introduce everyone and have a picnic in Princes Street Gardens.

There's a small voice inside my head asking what can possibly go wrong. And another one that keeps saying *everything*. I'm choosing to ignore it.

CHAPTER TWENTY

We're on the train to Edinburgh. I'm sitting beside Ed and we're facing Lauren. Her blonde hair is spread across her shoulders, and her pink-lipsticked mouth puckered sideways. I know she's chewing the inside of her cheek, just like she does every time she's nervous.

'What kind of stuff does your friend's dad paint?'

I'm not holding Ed's hand. I feel a bit shy, and also I don't want Lauren to feel like a third wheel, and we're all making stiff conversation as if we've just been introduced in an incredibly awkward social setting. Which we have.

'Um . . .' I think of the huge canvases layered with geometric shapes and colours. 'They're not really of *things* – they're more like . . . ideas.'

'I like paintings that look recognizable,' Lauren says. 'Like Monet and the impressionists.'

Their pretty floral art is as far removed from Jack's enormous in-your-face paintings as you can get. This is going to be a disaster.

'Well, they're – not that.'

Ed laughs. 'I think the idea is we're making up numbers. They want people there so it looks like lots of potential buyers are interested.'

Lauren giggles at this. 'Because we're totally the sort of people who'd be buying modern art.'

'I happen to be a bit of a connoisseur, actually,' Ed says in a silly mock-pompous voice. 'I've got several artworks in my bedroom.'

'I'm doing History of Art as a Higher.' Lauren fiddles with the cuff of her shirt.

'Me too,' Ed says.

And somehow that breaks the ice, and the rest of the journey we compare notes on the awfulness of school and the hopes we have that fifth year might not be so bad. And I watch Ed and Lauren talking and think how weird this all is. But it feels good.

'You might need to work on your "polite but interested" gallery face,' Ed says to Lauren. 'Have you ever been to anything like this before?'

I shove him with my elbow. 'Could you sound any more patronizing?'

'It's fine.' Lauren laughs at him. 'I mean, if we didn't have you here mansplaining art, we mightn't know what we were looking at.'

'I didn't mean –' Ed's tone is mock-injured.

'I know,' we both say.

'You can't help it,' I continue. 'It's the patriarchy. Not your fault.'

'I can't win here, outnumbered by you two.'

Lauren and I exchange a look and grin at him. 'Nope.'

*

When we get to the gallery, my stomach is a tight knot of nerves and anxiety. This is so far out of my comfort zone that I have literally no point of reference. I'm not exactly an expert at smoothing over social situations, and I want everyone to get on. I feel like it's up to me to make it work. But Allie and Rio are standing at the back wall, chatting to his dad. Lauren peers at one of the paintings in the window.

'Ed,' she says, turning to him with a mischievous expression, 'can you just explain this painting to me?'

So when Allie and Rio spot us and hurtle to the front of the gallery, expecting just to be introduced to Ed, they're completely thrown to discover me and Lauren laughing, and Ed standing beside us with his hands in his pockets, shaking his head in despair.

'You must be Ed,' says Rio, and puts his hand out. Working here has turned him into the version of himself he always wanted to be. He's in a skinny black tie and a shirt, and the grey suit he bought ages ago from the charity shop in town. Somehow he carries it off.

'Thank God,' Ed says. 'These two are ganging up on me.'

And Rio looks at us, and Lauren straightens up, and for a second there's a weird feeling in the air. He and Allie haven't been around to see the transformation of Lauren into someone I'd voluntarily spend time with . . . or the re-transformation? Whatever. I really hoped that when school went back, she wasn't going to go back to being the ice queen of the popular gang, and us to the pond slime social rejects.

We do all the introductions. Allie's still un-prickly and genuinely delighted to meet Ed, dragging him across the room to meet Rio's dad. I watch her as she flicks her pale pink hair over her shoulder. It's grown this summer. She looks happy. I watch as her face lights up and she gives a tiny, shy wave to a girl who has just walked past us in the doorway.

'Love's young dream, strike two,' says Rio, rolling his eyes at Lauren.

And for a weird fleeting moment as I watch Allie greeting Milly with a kiss – because this is a gallery in Edinburgh and not the high street in Kilmuir – I think that if this was a movie, it would end with Lauren the High School Princess getting together with Rio the Sharp-suited Outcast. But he takes her off to look at the paintings, and I think that with Rio explaining them maybe they'll make some sense, at least.

Ed catches my eye and saunters across the room towards me, taking two glasses of white wine as he passes the table.

'We can't have that,' I say, taking it anyway.

'Watch me.' Ed downs his in a gulp. 'God, that's disgusting. I have no idea why anyone drinks wine. Want another?'

'OK,' I say, and when he comes back I tip the contents of one of my glasses into the other so it's full almost to the top.

'I don't want you lot rolling home pissed,' says Jack, in passing. 'I'll be the one who gets it in the neck.'

'I'll make sure he behaves,' I say.

Ed raises his eyebrows at me. 'Shame,' he says, and pulls me close so the wine glass sloshes slightly, making a puddle on the floor.

'Stop it.' We're in a gallery and I want to kiss him, but I'm aware that we're right in the middle of the floor and everyone's going to see us. And then I realize that maybe I should be a bit more like Allie, so I lean over and do it. Ed's eyebrows shoot up in surprise.

'We could always go for a walk,' he says. 'I bet Lauren will be fine here.'

'I can't leave her in the middle of a gallery with a load of random strangers and say, "Sorry, be right back – just going to go and do kissing," can I?'

'I don't know.' Ed grins. 'That sounds pretty good to me.'

I shake my head. 'You are a disgrace.'

'That's why you love me . . .'

And everything stops for a second as he realizes what he's said, and I look him in the eye for a second, and then look away and feel my cheeks stinging pink. And I wonder again how I'll know if I do. Or when. And –

'If you two lovebirds are up for it, we're thinking of heading over to the gardens in half an hour? Allie's got a load of stuff for a picnic, and Dad says we can take some of the food from out back.'

We're brought back to reality by Rio.

'Lauren's quite nice, really,' he continues, lowering his voice. 'I'm surprised.'

'She's my sister,' I say, hearing the unfamiliar words

242

coming out of my mouth and liking them. 'Of course she's nice.'

'You've got a point there.'

We sprawl on the grass in the gardens with the ever-present sound of bagpipes in the air. There's the rushing noise of traffic to one side, and the rumble of trains heading into Waverley station on the other, and the sky is a sharp bright blue above our heads.

Milly has brought a picnic blanket and we've laid all the food out on it. Ed swats a wasp away and rolls over on his side, putting his chin in his hand to look at me. I'm sitting cross-legged on the grass beside him. Lauren and Rio are looking at something on her phone.

'That's my dad's office, y'know.' Ed points to an imposing-looking building in the distance. 'Weird to think that right now he's up there, looking out at the gardens, not knowing I'm down here.'

I don't know what to say. I've never had a dad, and I've never really allowed myself to think about how it would feel to have one that actually bothered to stick around. And I look at Ed and notice there's a thoughtful expression on his face and his eyebrows are gathering in a frown.

'I think –' he springs to his feet – 'maybe I'll go and tell him what I think.'

I scramble up too. 'You can't do that.'

'Why not?' Ed brushes grass from his jeans.

I realize that the two glasses of wine he's had have given

243

him some sort of weird Dutch courage.

'Because you said yourself he's a master at manipulation and he hit your mum.'

I turn to enlist Lauren and Rio in persuading him it's a bad idea, but they're deep in conversation, and they don't even know the whole story.

'It's only a ten-minute walk from here. I'll just nip along and go to reception, tell them I want a word.'

'He might not be there.' I cross my fingers hopefully.

'Oh, I'm sure he will be. He's a workaholic. And if I show up, he'll stop what he's doing to *be there* for me. He likes to be seen to do the right thing.' A bitter expression crosses Ed's face.

I think about his mum in the little cottage with hardly any furniture, and about Ed stealing back her jewellery and meeting up with his cousin on the sly to try and sort things out. And I think about the huge house they left behind and the life they used to live. And I know Ed says he's happier now, but there's a part of me that wonders if he'd still take it all back, if his dad agreed to just walk out of the house and give them everything. And Lauren and I talked about it, and she said that his dad would have to give his mum half in the divorce, but that it didn't always work out like that. Sometimes the good guys don't win in the end, she'd said, and I'd thought of her living in that huge house with her dad and Clare and how she'd seemed happier living in our crappy little terrace than she'd ever been with her dad. Maybe being the good guy doesn't always mean walking away with everything . . .

'I'm coming with you,' I say to Ed, and I put my hand in his.

'He's an arsehole,' he warns me.

'It's fine. I've met plenty of them.'

I tell Lauren we'll be back in half an hour. She starts to ask where we're going, but I just say I'll explain later, and she nods.

We march up the streets past the Bank buildings and through flocks of suit-wearing businessmen. And then we arrive at the huge glass doors of Ed's father's office, and he presses the buzzer.

'I'm here to see my dad,' he says to an immaculately made-up receptionist.

I look at my scruffy shoes on the pristine wooden floor and feel like I've been dragged in from a pile of leftovers.

'Ed,' she says, looking up and smiling warmly. 'Haven't seen you round here for a while. How's school?'

Ed nods politely. 'Good, thanks.'

She asks us to take a seat, and brings us some fizzy water in coloured glasses. My mouth feels dry and I swallow the whole glass in one go.

Ed jiggles his knee up and down.

The lift opens, and we both jump up to standing.

A woman with a briefcase steps out and flicks her hair over one shoulder, jingling a set of keys in her hand.

We sit down again and wait.

Ten minutes pass, in which time neither of us says anything. I check the clock above the receptionist's head every thirty seconds and wonder what Lauren and Rio are doing now.

I'm halfway through a message to her when the lift bell rings, and the door opens again, and my stomach is whirling with nerves. Ed stands up and takes my hand, pulling me to upright. I can feel his palms are damp.

'I got your note,' says his father.

He's tall, taller even than Ed – he must be six foot five at least. His hair is really dark brown and brushed up with something so he looks even taller. And he grins at us, holding out his hand.

'I'm Mark Jarvis,' he says, and he shakes my hand, vigorously. 'This must be –'

And he turns to Ed, waiting for him to fill in my name.

'I'm Holly,' I say, sharply.

'Nice to meet you, Holly,' he says, smiling. 'Good to see you, son,' he says, when Ed doesn't speak.

And he tries to pull him into an awkward embrace, but Ed hasn't let go of my hand, so we end up in an ungainly tangle. I step backwards and so does Ed.

'Shall we get some lunch?'

I don't know what to do with any of this. I was expecting Ed to scream at him or shout or punch him, or for his dad to launch into a furious tirade about the fact we'd stolen the jewellery. I was not expecting him to be pleasantly charming and slightly uncomfortable.

Ed shakes his head. 'I don't have long.'

'Jane will sort us a room,' his dad says, and strides over to the receptionist.

I look at Ed and hope that my expression says everything. I seem to have been struck dumb by the weirdness of the situation.

'Right,' Ed's dad says, walking ahead of us and turning and beckoning for us to follow, 'we're in here.'

He holds open the door to a room where there's a huge table lined with expensive-looking chairs and a whiteboard at the end.

'I'm in here for a meeting later,' he says to me, smiling as if to try to put me at ease. He goes to a fancy-looking phone with lots of buttons and presses some kind of loudspeaker thing that connects him to Jane.

'Coffee and muffins, please, lovely,' he says into the air.

There's a second's pause and then Jane's voice comes back through the little speaker. 'Coming up.'

When he's finished, he looks up at us, smiling again.

'Can we just cut the bullshit?'

Ed blurts the words out angrily. He doesn't take the chair he's been offered, and I feel awkward sitting there while Ed is standing up beside me. But I can't work out how to get up or what to do.

'What are you talking about?' Ed's dad smiles at me as if trying to get me on side. 'Do you know what this is about?'

I open my mouth, but no words come out.

'You know we've got a new house?'

Ed pushes the back of the chair next to me angrily so it bangs on the table. I shove mine backwards and stand up, so I'm by his side.

'I heard, yes.'

'No thanks to you.'

'Ed, this isn't anything to do with us. Your mother and I splitting up – it's . . . I don't want to be painted as the bad guy in all of this . . .'

He tails off and looks at me again.

'The bad guy?' Ed spits. 'You treated her like shit for years. Made her feel like she was worthless.'

'Your mother can fight her own battles.'

'Really?'

Ed's eyes are blazing with anger now. His dad is torn between trying to fight his corner and appearing to be the kind, reasonable person in all of this to me.

'I think this isn't the time to be discussing it,' he begins, and the receptionist walks into the room, pushing the door with her hip, a tray in her hands.

'Here you are, Mark.' She smiles at him and puts down a coffee pot, three mugs, and a plate of chocolate muffins.

'Thanks,' he says, his manners impeccable. 'Appreciate it.'

Ed gives a snort of disgust, and she looks at him curiously. She smooths down her pencil skirt and turns to Ed's dad for direction. As far as she's concerned, he's the one in charge here.

'Teenagers,' his father says, with a too-loud laugh.

He gets up to see her out. As he does so, Ed stands up and walks across the room so I'm between the two of them. He's standing at the top of the table, in the space where his father stood a few moments ago.

I turn and realize in that moment that I'm caught between the two of them, and I feel a chill despite the warmth of the summer day. His dad's shoulders seem to reach almost from one side of the doorframe to the other. He's built like a rugby player with huge, broad hands.

I think of Ed's mum, Lucy, and how sweet and kind she is, and I imagine how it must have felt to be hit by him. I feel bile and fear rising in my throat.

I turn to look at Ed, and put a hand to my mouth.

'You OK?' Ed turns to me, gentle for a second.

'Mmm.' I nod, keeping my lips pressed together.

His father doesn't say anything. He carefully adjusts the cufflinks on his shirt and looks at us. His face doesn't register any emotion at all for a moment, as if he's a snake trying to calculate how best to attack his prey. I feel my heart thudding in my ears.

'I don't know what shit your mother has been filling your head with, but she's more than capable of fighting her own battles.' His face settles into a smile, which doesn't meet his eyes, and his voice has a cold, flat tone that sends another chill up my spine.

'So why aren't you paying her any money?'

Ed's father gives a shake of his head, as if he's a silly child.

'Of course I'm going to be paying her money,' he says, faux-patiently. 'We're just waiting for the legal details to be sorted.'

'And in the meantime we're meant to survive on nothing?' Ed's jaw lifts as he speaks.

'That was never my intention.'

Ed's father steps towards the table, and I take a step back without meaning to.

'Let's have a coffee; we can talk about this. This is just a silly misunderstanding between your mother and me. If you want money, all you have to do is ask your mother to speak to me in person, like I've asked her to, and we can sort this nonsense out.'

I can feel Ed's body going rigid as his dad calmly pours coffee into three mugs. He holds one out to me. I raise a hand at him to say, *No, thank you. No, I don't want your coffee. You give me the creeps.*

'Your mother's no angel,' he begins. He adds milk and three sugars, stirring his coffee for a long time. There's no other noise in the room except the sound of the spoon clattering against the edges of the mug. 'I don't know why you are painting me to be the monster when she's just as bad. It was just a silly misunderstanding, which she's blown out of all proportion.'

I feel so uncomfortable. He keeps saying it over and over again. A silly misunderstanding. As if he's trying to convince himself as well as us. Ed's almost gone white with rage, and I know we've got to leave.

'Come on, Ed,' he begins, softening his tone. 'Don't you want your old life back? Your house, your things, your school –' he looks at me pointedly – 'your real friends?'

Ed suddenly takes me by the hand and pushes past the chairs so we circle the big table and head for the door. His dad steps forward and for a moment I think he's about to block our way and I feel my stomach churning again.

But he steps back.

'A silly misunderstanding?' Ed spits at him. 'You hit my

250

mother. You ground her down every single day. Told her she was worthless. You mocked her and told me she was insane. I don't want my old life back. All this –' he motions to the posh furniture and the huge windows that look out over the city – 'you can keep it.'

And I look his father in the eye, and he looks back at me, and I don't know what it is I see there, but I don't think it's regret that he's hurt his son. It looks more like he's angry he's been exposed for what he is. Ed pulls me out, slamming the door behind us, and we march out into the foyer. The receptionist is there and she looks up. Her face is white.

'Ed, tell your mum I'm here if she needs me.' Her voice is low, but determined. 'If there's anything I can do. *Anything.*'

I give her a brief, confused smile.

We sit down on a concrete block that's just outside the office, and I take Ed's hand in mine.

'Did that help?' I say quietly.

Ed shakes his head. 'Not really. I needed to see him face to face – I thought if he saw me he would realize the harm he's done and apologize. But there was nothing.'

'I'm sorry.'

'S'OK.' He lifts his hand to mine and holds it up so our fingers touch, and he doesn't say anything for a moment. Then he laces his fingers through mine and holds on, tightly and starts to quietly laugh.

I turn and look at him. It's the relief of getting it over

with, I think, that's making him laugh.

'I think I was expecting I'd go in there and he'd say, "You know what? You're right – I'm an abusive arsehole. Here's the house and all the money,"' he says. 'But the second I saw him I realized that he was never going to do that.'

Ed's eyes are blazing bright, and he looks like he's just won something.

'Didn't you see? When he was closing the door behind Jane, I pressed the button on that fancy phone thing, so she could hear every word. He's not going to change, but if he's not going to make this easy, neither am I. He's a dick, and now everyone who works for him will hear about it, one way or another.'

I think of his dad going back into the room and noticing, and I wish I could see his face.

'But you haven't sorted anything out.'

'Yet.' Ed smiles at me and squeezes my hand. He pushes the hair out of his face. 'We'll be OK. And I don't want my old life back. I happen to quite like my new one, weirdly enough.'

We cram into Rio's dad's Land Rover and sing along to his terrible music all the way home. We drop off Ed first, and I climb out to let him out and laugh as he untangles his long legs from the back of the truck.

'I'll see you,' he says, and drops a kiss on my temple.

I squeeze his hand and watch from the back window as we drive away. He lopes down the front path of the cottage, and the door opens as his mum greets him. He turns and raises an arm in farewell just as we turn out of sight.

EPILOGUE

'You lot are going to get me sacked,' Cressi yells across the water of the pool.

I throw a float at her from the water and duck under before she can launch it back at me. I dive down, pulling myself through the blueness of the water, listening to the echoes above me, and then I swim up to the surface. The last of the evening sun is shining through the skylights and reflecting on the surface, so the dappled light dips and sparkles everywhere.

'Are you going to ask Cressi if she'll come up to the woods with us?'

Ed's treading water in the deep end beside me. He puts out an arm and holds on to the edge of the pool, and he catches my hand, pulling me through the water. I push wet hair out of my face and shake away the drops of water that are running down my forehead. He swirls me round so I'm pressed up against the wall of the pool and he has his arms on either side of me and the only thing holding me up is him and I let out a gasp of surprise as he kisses me. And when he stops I realize that despite the cool of the water I can feel the warmth of his skin against mine.

'Do you think she'd be up for it?' I look across the pool at Cressi.

'She's pretty game, our Cressida.' Ed laughs. 'I'll ask her.'

And I watch as he cuts through the water and vaults out at the other side, standing in front of her. I can see her laughing and shaking her head no, and I know what she's saying – you don't need me there, you young things – and I can see Ed insisting that she comes, his big grin spread across his face, and he's nodding.

'Holly!' Lauren's balanced on the top of an inflatable slide, her blonde hair tied back in a ponytail. As I wave to her she topples off backwards and falls into the water, emerging with a massive smile on her face.

Allie and Rio are messing about in an inflatable boat at the other side of the deep end. We've been setting up for the end-of-summer pool party that's taking place tomorrow morning. I think when Cressi invited me to get the others to come and help she wasn't visualizing a bunch of sixteen-year-olds acting like primary-school kids let loose after exam time, but she's taking it in reasonably good spirit.

We're heading to the woods with a portable barbecue and a packet of marshmallows later. Allie's nicked some beers from the shop – some things never change – and I'm pretty certain she'll be in trouble when her parents work out they're missing. But I don't think they'll be *that* worried.

I sit on the edge of the pool and watch everyone and

wonder how my life could change so much in the course of one summer. How I realized that I don't have to keep everything stored in a box to keep it safe. Our house isn't spotless now, but Mum's still singing and playing music, and she's signed up to start teaching music again when school starts. And we're going to Norfolk next Easter to see all her old band friends. Lauren's coming too – she's half hoping she'll hook up with a rock star's offspring and end up in *Heat* magazine, I think.

Ed's mum is working in the women's centre, and his dad's still being a dick – he's hired a super-expensive lawyer to make sure he gets as much as he can out of the divorce, but there's a rumour that there's a sexual harassment case being made against him by several of the women at work, so I get the feeling that karma's going to get him in the end.

Allie and Milly are still going strong and making plans for a flat in Edinburgh when Allie finishes her exams this year – and Rio's decided against going back to school at all. He's got an apprenticeship in a design studio and bought himself the sharpest suit he could find for his first day.

And I've given up on being invisible. I've joined the swimming team, even though the idea of competing with everyone watching terrifies me. But this summer has taught me a lot.

I stand up and swing my arms, springing from the edge of the pool and curving through the air. I'm ready.

The End

INFORMATION

According to the most recent figures from the Office for National Statistics, two women are killed each week by a current or former partner, and an estimated 1.2 million women have suffered domestic abuse in the last year.

If you need help or support
Freephone 24-Hour National Domestic Violence
Helpline: **0808 2000 247**
    run in partnership with **Women's Aid** and **Refuge**

refuge.org.uk
Refuge say they are 'Committed to a world where domestic violence and violence against women and girls is not tolerated and where women and children can live in safety.

We aim to empower women and children to rebuild their lives, free from violence and fear. We provide a range of life-saving and life-changing services, and a voice for the voiceless.'

womensaid.org.uk

Women's Aid say 'Everyone has the human right to live in safety and free from violence and abuse. Society has a duty to recognise and defend this right. Women are the overwhelming majority of victims of domestic abuse. Domestic abuse is a violation of women and their children's human rights. It is the result of an abuse of power and control, and is rooted in the historical status and inequality of women in in society.'

The leading UK charity **Mind** says 'In its mildest form, depression can mean just being in low spirits. It doesn't stop you leading your normal life but makes everything harder to do and seem less worthwhile. At its most severe, depression can be life-threatening because it can make you feel suicidal or simply give up the will to live.'

Every year, one in four people will experience a mental health problem.

For information, advocacy and support, visit: **mind.org.uk**

For a kind word, support, and understanding, as well as self-care strategies for even the hardest days, **The Blurt Foundation** are a social enterprise dedicated to helping people affected by depression. Visit: **blurtitout.org**

ACKNOWLEDGEMENTS

There were times when I was writing this book when I thought it was never going to end – it turns out that when you write your second book in a new genre, you can have second book syndrome all over again. That was an unexpected delight. But I loved Holly and Ed, and I knew that their story was one that really mattered to me, so I'm delighted to be finally writing the thank-you bit.

Firstly a huge thanks to Rachel Petty, my brilliant editor – for edit notes that make me laugh (snogzzz) and cry (oh my god you want me to do MORE?) and for pushing me to make this the very best book it could be. And to Amanda Preston my agent, for being kind and saying 'no you are NOT the author from hell' when I call you for the twelfth time in a week saying THIS IS IMPOSSIBLE. You are both wonderful. Sorry I'm such a drama queen.

To everyone at Team MKB – you are amazing and I'm so proud and happy to be published by you. Thank you for your kindness and humour and general fabulosity.

To the writing wolf pack – Alice, Hayley, and Keris – I love you all, you make my life better every single day. Everyone should have funny, feminist friends who use lots of words beginning with f.

To the literary hooters, Miranda, Jo and Cathy – thank you for always having my back. I love you lot.

To Elise, who's been my best friend since I was eight, and who introduced me to Judy Blume – love you and thank you for always being there. To my dear friends Anne, Shirley and Carol for making me cry at a book launch – please do it again soon. And to Jax and Aimee, who cheered me from start to finish as I wrote – thank you for keeping me (relatively) sane. And to Rhi, because I love you.

To all the amazing book bloggers and the #ukya gang who cheer on our books and make it such a lovely place to be – on and off line – thank you for being brilliant.

I would like to thank John Taylor, who bid in the Authors for Grenfell auction to raise money for the survivors of the Grenfell Tower fire. His name is featured in this book as a thank you.

Thanks also to Cressi Downing who was the winning bidder in the CLIC Sargent Get in Character Auction, and whose name features in the book.

To my family, for being funny and because I love them, even when I don't return their calls because I'm writing (or editing, or one of the other million excuses I have for being hopelessly disorganised . . .)

To Ross – I couldn't do this without you. Thank you for everything, but most of all for making me laugh every single day. Also: I love you.

To Verity, Archie, Jude and Rory – you are amazing. I love you millions. Do you mind if we just have pasta?

Hahahaha xxxxx

And to Mabel and Martha, you amazing woofers: thank you for being the best dogs ever. I look forward to you eating a copy of this book to demonstrate your appreciation.

And last of all, to you. Reading this. Whether it's at home, at school, in a library* or you're sneaking a read in the bookshop and trying to decide if you should choose this one. Thank you for reading this when you could be doing a million other things.

*Libraries are AMAZING. Use them, support them, and tell everyone else to do the same. Free books: what could be better?

ABOUT THE AUTHOR

Rachael Lucas is an author, coach and freelance writer. Her bestselling debut novel, *Sealed with a Kiss*, has been downloaded over 130,000 times on Kindle. She lives and works in a Victorian house by the seaside in the north-west of England with her partner (also a writer) and their children.

AUTHOR'S NOTE

Growing up in Scotland it always felt to me that books were magical things written by far-away people, and – apart from a few exceptions – they were all set in England. So, I knew when I started writing Holly and Ed's story that I wanted it to be set somewhere that made sense to me, in a setting that reminded me of my own childhood.

I lived in little white house on an estate just like Holly's house. I played on the same streets she talks about, and I caught the same bus from our little town on the Firth of Forth up to the next town where the railway station was. My town was called Bo'ness, and the next-door town was Linlithgow. If you know the area, you'll recognise the setting – and the loch, and Linlithgow Palace where Mary Queen of Scots was born. I've changed the town names because it's not *quite* the same – but I've kept the historical details. And I hope that if you're growing up in a little town where nothing much happens you'll read this and see that if you fall in love with telling stories when you're at school, you can grow up and make it your job, too.

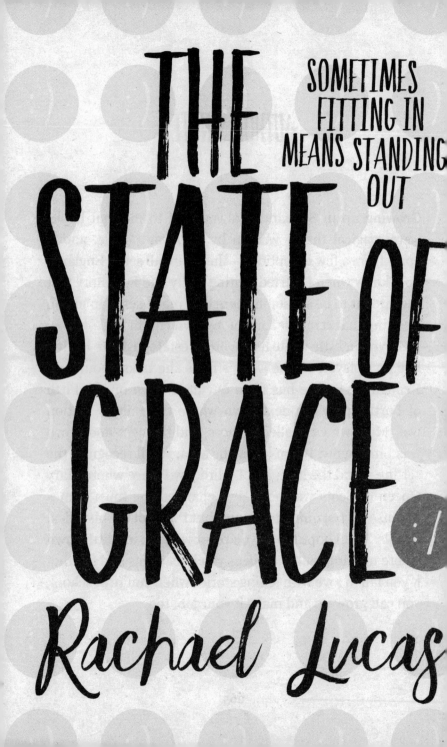

THE STATE OF GRACE

SOMETIMES FITTING IN MEANS STANDING OUT

:/

Rachael Lucas